Choices
Men Make

Also by
Dwayne S. Joseph

Choices Men Make

The Womanizers

Never Say Never

Anthology:
Around the Way Girls
A Dollar and a Dream
Gigolos Get Lonely Too

Choices Men Make

Dwayne S. Joseph

URBAN BOOKS LLC
www.urbanbooks.com

Urban Books
10 Brennan Place
Deer Park, NY 11729

ISBN 1-893196-60-7

First Printing August 2006
Printed in the United States of America

10 9 8 7 6 5 4 3 2 1

Submit Wholesale Orders to:
Kensington Publishing Corp.
C/O Penguin Group (USA) Inc.
Attention: Order Processing
405 Murray Hill Parkway
East Rutherford, NJ 07073-2316
Phone: 1-800-526-0275
Fax: 1-800-227-9604

Acknowledgments

God: Thank you. This was when you made my dream a reality.

Thanks to my wife, Wendy, and my little girls, Tatiana & Natalia. I love you.

Thanks to the entire Urban Books staff.

To my friends and family: Love you guys!!

A BIG thank you to the readers and book clubs. This is the one that started it all. Enjoy.

Watch out for my new novel, *If Your Girl Only Knew.*

To my New York Giants: The Super Bowl is coming! Let's keep it going!!

Peace,

Dwayne S. Joseph
www.Dwaynesjoseph.com
Djoseph21044@yahoo.com

Roy Burges

1

"**M**y boys! What uuuuuup? I didn't think you two were brave enough to show up. Are you guys sure you want to see my Titans kick the Redskins' no-game-winning ass?" I stepped to the side to let Vic and Colin step in. Behind them trailed Vic's wife, Julie, and some date of Colin's that I'd never seen before. Both women had the same blasé look that my wife, Stacey, gave me whenever I mentioned *football*.

"What's up, Julie?" I kissed her on the cheek.

"Hey, Roy." She kissed me back. "Where's Stacey?"

"She's hiding in the kitchen."

"Well, as much as I'd love to see the football game . . ." Julie winked.

I smiled and looked at Colin's date. She looked no more than 25, with maroon highlights in her light-brown hair.

I extended my hand. "Roy Burges."

She looked at my hand and cleared her throat loudly.

Colin, who was taking off his coat, chuckled. "Oh, my bad. Roy, this is Tanecia. Tanecia, Roy."

Tanecia smiled half-heartedly then shook my hand.

"Come on, Tanecia"—Julie took her by the hand—"let's go help Stacey hide in the kitchen," and waved as they stepped past me.

I closed the door and looked at Vic, who looked back at me and shook his head.

Colin had done it again. Probably hooked up with her last night at some club or bar, bought her a couple of drinks, used a couple of "Mac" lines, and then took her back to his place, where he would later enter her name into his "book of conquests."

Colin and relationships went together like fire and ice; in other words, it just wasn't happening. Somewhere within his warped mind was the belief that women were good for only casual sex; marriage and commitment were out of the question. "I'm a committed bachelor for life," he always said. As long as I'd known him, I'd never seen him come close to having any type of meaningful relationship.

I gave my boys a pound as we walked into the living room. "So what's up, fellas? You ready to see your boys lose or what?" Being a Titans fan from Tennessee, I was enjoying the dismal season the Redskins were having. The Titans were enjoying a 4-1 record, while the Redskins were stuck at 0-5.

Vic sat down on the sofa and shook his head.

"Man, there will be no loss for us today. This is our week."

"Vic, why do you refuse to accept the truth?" I looked at him and shook my head. "The Redskins suck. What in the hell makes you think the outcome of today's game is going to be any different from the last five?" I sucked my teeth and looked over at Colin. "So what's up, Colin? You and this unfortunate fool over here in cahoots? You think the Redskins are pulling this one out too?"

Colin raised an eyebrow and looked at his boy. "Vic," he said as he sat in my inflatable chair with the Titans logo on it, "you my dog and all, and the Redskins are my team, but I can't go with you on this one. The Titans are gonna kick our sorry asses all over Sunday."

"Ha! ha!" I laughed, sitting in my beanbag. "At least someone has some sense."

Vic, wearing his Darrell Green jersey, mumbled and pounded on his chest. "I'm tellin' you two fools this is our day. I bet sixty bucks on this game. You know when I bet money we win."

"Kid," Colin said, "you could have just given that sixty to me—I would have shown a freak a good time with that."

We laughed and then got serious as the game began. We had our game faces on. This, and pool on Wednesday nights, was our weekly ritual. During the football season, we always got together at each other's place on Sundays to watch the game. This week was my turn to play host, which wasn't a hard thing to do, considering all I needed to do was buy a case of Heineken and a couple bags of chips.

Julie, Stacey, and whichever date Colin decided to bring, if anyone, usually did just what they were doing as the game was on—they sat in the kitchen and gossiped.

After the first quarter, the Titans had a 14-point lead; by halftime, the lead was 21. I looked at my two depressed friends and shook my head. "Damn, it's quiet in here." I smiled.

"Whatever." Vic stared at the television screen.

I laughed and looked to the kitchen, where the women had hibernated, then looked back at Colin. "So what's up with this Tanecia, man? She somebody? Is it possible that you may have found someone worthy?"

"Roy, please . . ." Colin's eyes widened. "The only thing she's worthy of is a star beside her name. I hooked up with her at 1223 in DC last night. She was all over me. Dog, I smacked that ass 'nuff times on the dance floor; she had it just poised for me to do it. Yo, I knew when she let me do that, I wasn't going home alone."

"Colin, man, why are you always hooking up with some freak? Don't you want anything real?" Vic asked.

"'Real'? *You* better get real. *Sheeeit.* Just 'cause you're married now, don't mean I need to be gettin' tied down. You guys know me. You know I'm not about no commitment—all I want is a freak at night, and to be left alone in the morning."

"That'll get tired, man," I said.

"For who? Surely you don't mean for me. That will never happen. You guys like that marriage shit, not me. I couldn't handle that—waking up next to the same woman day after day, eating the same pie day after day, hearing the nagging day after day. Nah, you fools can have that drama; I'll keep my bachelorhood."

I couldn't help laughing. He hadn't changed a bit.

I remember when Colin and I met. He came in to Carmax looking to trade in his Nissan Maxima, which was in immaculate condition.

When he walked in, he wasted no time. He stepped up to me before I had a chance to go into my salesman spiel. "You helpin' anybody?"

"No." I was glad to have finally snagged a customer. I had just moved from Tennessee with Stacey to take the job with Carmax, so my clientele list was pretty much non-existent. I extended my hand. "Roy Burges. What can I do for you?"

"Colin," he said, shaking my hand. "I need a new car, Roy." He took a quick glance at his watch.

"Pressed for time?" I wondered whether he was there to browse and waste my time, or to actually drive off with something new and put money in my pocket.

"Always pressed for time, Roy."

"Okay. Well, are you looking for a brand-new car or something used?"

"Brand-new, Roy. Always brand-new—for the ladies, you know."

I nodded. "I got you."

"Good. Let's find a ride I can do some mackin' in."

"Well, are you looking for anything in particular?"

Colin thought for a second and then said, "I want something black and smooth, with all the necessary accessories—I want a carbon copy of me." He laughed out loud. "Just kiddin', dog."

I laughed and shook my head. I could tell that he had no problem with his self-esteem. "Okay, well tell me this—are you looking for a sports car, a luxury car, or an SUV?"

"Had the combo of luxury and sports in my Maxima. I want an SUV this time. Speaking of Maxima, I have it outside; I want to trade it in."

"Okay, well let's get the appraisal going for that and then start looking at some SUV's." When we went into the parking lot to his car, I asked in disbelief. "You want to trade this in?" The Maxima was loaded: tinted windows, 20" chrome rims, and a spoiler on the back. The inside was just as clean, with shining leather interior, and a carpet so spotless, it looked like no one ever set foot on it. I looked at my reflection in the gleaming waxed black paint and said, "This thing is bad. You really want to trade this in?"

Colin laughed. "Man, I've had this thing for two years. I need something new, dog—I can't let the ladies see me in the same car for too long, know what I mean?"

"You always make your decisions based on women?"

"Dog, what else?"

I laughed and shook my head. "Okay, if you really want to trade it in . . ." I filled out some paperwork and put a yellow cone on top of the car to have it appraised.

Colin and I went to the lot where the new cars

were. It didn't take him long to find the car he wanted—it was actually the first one we looked at. "This is it!" Colin said. He walked around the Isuzu Rodeo and rubbed his hands together as if he were plotting something. "Dog, when the honeys see me in this—yo, let's get that paperwork going."

"You don't want to look at anything else?" I asked.

"Roy, this the one."

"Okay, let's get that paperwork started."

We went inside, filled out all the necessary forms, and got the trade-in value for the Maxima. As we waited for a response from the banks for financing, we sat in my office and talked about his many adventures in the Nissan.

"Dog, I'ma miss that car."

"Yeah, I bet—Maximas' are reliable."

"Damn skippy they are! I could always rely on that car to pick me up a honey. Dog, I had so many escapades and inspected so much pussy in that car, I should have changed the license plate to *O-B-G-Y-N*."

I busted out laughing. Colin was amusing, to say the least. It was nice to actually deal with a customer who not only wanted a car, but was also fun to talk to.

"So what do you do, Mr. *O-B-G-Y-N*?" I asked.

"I have my own software company. Ever heard of IBIS?"

"Don't think so. What kind of software?"

"You know the system the mechanics use in your service area?"

"Not too well."

"Well, that's my software; actually, *our* software. I started IBIS with my brother about three years ago; Carmax was one of our first customers."

"Damn! that's cool."

"Yeah. But we don't just do the software for mechanics. We do software for anybody that wants to keep track of their inventory, ring up sales, order supplies, keep updated records and files, anything. You tell us what you want to do, and we can create software for you to do it with."

"Sounds lucrative."

"Roy, dog, you have no idea. We're blowin' up. And we're going after the big boys. We want to take on the record stores next. Do you know there is only one major software program record stores use to keep track of everything going on? One! And it's outdated; at least compared to our program it is. We're creating software that a fool could use. It's in testing right now, but once it's out—*cha-ching*!"

"That's good, man. Real good. Nice to see brothers doing well."

"Only way to do it, man. So what's your story? I see all of these plaques and awards you have here. You the top seller here or what?"

"Not yet," I said with a proud smile, "but I will be in time. These awards are from the dealership I worked it when I was in Tennessee. I just moved here with my wife and girls two months ago. I'm still in the process of building up my clientele here. But once I do, I figure I'll be a selling fool."

"Right, right. Tennessee, huh? I thought I heard a Southern accent. So that means you're a Titans fan?"

"Definitely!"

"Sorry to hear that. You may want to get hip to the Redskins."

"No way. I'm a Titans fan for life."

"We'll see. So two months, huh? And you're married? You know anyone here?"

"Nah. Just the wife and kids."

Colin looked at a picture of Stacey and my twin girls, Sheila and Jenea. "Twins, huh? Must be a handful?"

"And then some," I said proudly.

Colin nodded his head. "How old are they?"

"The one on the left in the red top is Sheila; she's three. Jenea, in blue, is older by three minutes."

"So what made you move here?"

"I wanted a change. Plus I'd heard good things about Maryland. I started looking at dealerships here and the salaries they offered, and I saw an opportunity to make a decent living here."

"Your wife didn't mind moving?"

"Nah, both of us wanted the change of scenery."

"Your wife work?"

"All the time—she takes care of the home and the girls—but she says she wants to learn to design web pages."

"Looks like I may have to talk to her one day. We could always use a fresh look for our web page."

"She'd be willing when she learns it. I just hope you wouldn't mind working with an amateur."

"Everyone's an amateur at some point; besides, we gotta support each other."

"I hear that."

"Well, that's cool." He reached for his wallet. "But we can't have you not knowing anybody— here's my card, dog; give me a holla. If your wife don't mind, I'll take you out sometime, show you what Maryland and DC have to offer."

I slid his card into my wallet. "That's cool. Just don't forget I'm married."

Colin laughed. "Roy, I promise not to corrupt you too much. "

We were interrupted by the sound of the beep on my PC. "The info's back from the banks," I said.

"What's the damage?" Colin asked.

After he settled on a financing offer and we crossed all t's and dotted all i's, I handed him the key to the Rodeo.

He got in his brand-new ride, removed a CD from his pocket, and slid it in. As Wu-Tang Clan blared from the speakers, Colin yelled, "Yeah, dog! I'm pullin' a honey tonight. Yo, hit me up; we'll hang."

"Will do."

"A'ight. I'm outta here." He turned the volume up even louder then drove off.

I smiled. It felt good to make that sale, but more importantly, it felt good to have finally met someone.

Since moving to Laurel, Maryland, I'd had no time for getting to know anyone. Stacey and I were too busy getting the house together and taking care of the girls. I wanted to get her a car, but she refused to drive even though she had a license. Years before I met her, she'd been involved in a head-on collision with another car. Her sister, whose picture she kept in a locket around her neck, died instantly. Stacey, who happened to be driving, came away with a broken leg and a few cuts and bruises and hadn't driven since, and so most of my free time was spent as a chauffeur.

I hooked up with Colin a few days after he bought the Rodeo. He cruised by my place and picked me up. Vic was with him when he came. We went to Club *U* in DC, where they played go-go music all night long. While Colin and Vic lurked around, running game on every fine sister that crossed their path, I stayed at the bar with a beer and soaked in the atmosphere.

Maryland's pace was much faster than that of Tennessee. The music, the style of dance, the clothing—they were all sharper. The women were different too; they seemed more aggressive. Even the white women were running their game on the brothers. Now that was something I definitely wasn't used to seeing. Although I personally had no real problem with it, the amount of interracial couples in the club was surprising. But even though the differences were a little intimidating, it still felt good being out, even if it felt a little awkward not being with Stacey.

Unlike most guys I knew, I enjoyed spending time with my wife. We met when we were both freshmen at Tennessee State University, where she was majoring in psychology, and I was majoring in business. Taken by her small, dark eyes, broad nose, full lips, and thick frame, I hounded her for a good month before she finally agreed to go out with me.

We started dating exclusively two weeks after our

first date. Our courtship lasted all of six months before we finally got married. Stacey was my soul mate, and I saw no reason to delay; she felt the same. The rest, as they say, is history.

We had Sheila and Jenea during our second year of marriage. Being with Stacey completed me in a way I'd always dreamed about. She was strong in all of my weak areas, and vice versa. That's why I was content keeping the bar company and listening to the go-go music, which was one style of music that I could do without.

Colin and Vic had known each other since junior high school, so their bond was already strong. But as time passed, they became the brothers I never had. Our personalities all gelled to form a circle of brotherhood that no one could break— we all had each other's backs. And when Vic, a white boy with more soul than OJ, eventually got married to Julie, Colin and I shared best man duties.

"A'ight, fellas," I said, rubbing my palms together and focusing back on the game, "second half's about to start. How many more points will my Titans score on that ass?" I swallowed down my beer and turned up the volume.

Colin laughed and shrugged his shoulders. Vic, who stared intensely at the screen, shook his head and kept a tight lip.

Roy

2

After the Titans' lopsided 36-point victory, Colin
left to take Tanecia home while Vic and Julie
stayed behind for a little while. As our wives continued to chitchat, Vic and I went to the basement
and shot a game of pool. As I sank the eight ball
for my third consecutive victory, I asked, "Man,
you think Colin will ever change?"

Vic chalked off his pool stick and shook his head.
"No way. As long as I've known him, that brother is
not about settling down. It would take an extremely
special freak to satisfy him."

"True, indeed. Although she was a bit standoffish,
that girl, Tanecia, seemed to be okay. And from what
I was seeing when we ate, it looks like she likes him."

"Man, all the women like Colin. That pretty boy
never had a problem with the women. Shit, Tanecia
can like him all she wants; it won't make a difference—she's still just another notch in his bedpost."

"You're definitely right about that."

"I know I am. He'll probably call her tonight and tell her he had a good time and hopes to do it again sometime. That'll get her all worked up. Then he'll call her once during the week. Probably tell her that he has to go away on business, but he'll call her when he gets back. Give it about two weeks, and he'll call again to say things have been so hectic that he's got no time to do anything but he wants to be friends."

"Yeah," I agreed. "In between that time, he'll have met at least two other freaks. *And* Tanecia will still be sweating him. The brother is definitely a player's player."

"Yeah," Vic said, hitting a nine-eleven combination in the corner pocket. "No doubt about that."

"It feels good to not have to be in the game like that, doesn't it?" I watched him miss a bank shot. "I mean, I know I am truly a lucky man to have Stacey by my side to keep me sane. And even if you don't admit it too, Nic, I know you feel the same about Julie. It's a relaxed feeling—being with the woman you want to spend the rest of your life with."

Vic stayed quiet and wrinkled his brow as I missed a combination.

I knew something was up. "Why aren't you speaking, Vic? You do feel lucky, don't you?" He moved to take his next shot. "Vic? What's up, man? Why aren't you saying anything?"

Vic put his stick down and stared at me with a sigh. In his eyes I saw the look of a troubled man.

"Aww, man, what's going on? Are you guys having problems?" I asked.

Vic looked toward the steps and then closed the

door to the upstairs. "Roy," he said in a voice just slightly above a whisper, "I don't think I can be married to Julie anymore."

It was my turn to put the stick down. "What? What do you mean, can't be married?"

"Man, this stays with you and me."

"Okay."

"I'm not happy."

"'Not happy'? What are you talking about?— You and Julie just got married six months ago; you're still supposed to be on your honeymoon."

"Keep your voice down. Just hear me out."

"I'm listening." I leaned my two-hundred-twenty-pound frame against the pool table.

"Man, you know why I married Julie. You know I was never really in love with her."

"Yeah, but you still said 'I do.' "

"Because I felt like I had to. Man, when she told me she was pregnant, I felt like I had no choice. I told you and Colin I wasn't trying to have that baby be born out of wedlock."

"Look, you made the decision to promise until death do you part. How can you just back out now?"

"Because, as much as I love Julie, I'm not head over heels in love with her."

"Who says you have to be 'head over heels'?"

"I do. I want to feel that kind of love that you feel, but I never will with Julie."

"How do you know?"

"Roy, I've always known. I was willing to sacrifice what I wanted for the baby's sake. I was determined to be in it for the long haul, but when she miscarried, I knew that I couldn't go on."

"So because she lost the baby, you feel like you have an out now? Vic, Julie loves you. She would do anything for you. How could you not love her like that?"

"Roy, listen. I know how Julie feels about me. But no matter how hard I try, I just don't feel the same about her."

"And you don't think that you can get to that point?"

"No, I don't. Honestly, man. And I've never told you and Colin this—but the real reason I'm not happy with Julie is because I love black women."

I stared at Vic for a quiet second and then doubled over laughing.

"Man, it's not funny. I'm serious. You know how I feel about black women, how I've always felt."

"Look, I know you love the sisters, and I'll admit, you were the last person I expected to date a white woman. But Julie is a good, attractive, loving woman. You can't deny that. So even though I was surprised that you ended up with her, it wasn't hard to see why. Now having said all of that, you can't really be serious about leaving her because you want a sister." I stared at Vic, looking for a sign that my logic had gotten through to him.

He sighed. "I can't do it, man."

"Come on, Vic. I mean—forget color—do you know how hard it is to find all of the qualities Julie has in one woman? Shit, I love black women too, but don't you think you're being a little ridiculous?"

"Roy, have you forgotten that I was adopted by a black woman when I was two? Or that I grew up in southeast DC? Man, I've lived around black women all my life. I never even thought of dating a white woman until I met Julie. And I just kind of fell into that. You know I never wanted marriage, but she got pregnant. I was trying to do the right thing. But as each day goes by, I just don't feel like I fit with her. She is a beautiful person, but she doesn't have the energy of a black woman that I need. She doesn't have the attitude."

"'Attitude'? You want attitude? Vic, are you hearing what you're saying?"

"I've been hearing it loud and clear. Man, I love the fire that black women have. I love their no-nonsense attitude. Julie does love me and would do anything for me, but that's a problem for me."

"'A problem'? Vic, are you high? How could a woman loving you and doing anything for you be a problem?"

"Man, let me show you something"—He walked up the stairs and opened the door—"Julie!" he said loudly.

"Yeah, babe?" Julie answered from the kitchen.

"Hey, can you bring a beer down here for me and Roy?" Vic came back down the stairs and stared at me without saying a word.

Thirty seconds later, Julie came down the steps with two beers in hand.

Vic kissed her on the cheek. "Thanks, babe," he said. When she disappeared upstairs and closed the door behind her, Vic gave me a beer, downed some of his, and kept his eyes locked on mine.

I took a sip and shrugged my shoulders. "And that's a problem for you?"

"Man, you ask Stacey to bring you a beer."

I sucked my teeth. "Shit! That ain't happening."

"Exactly. That's my point. I want that. I want that you-have-two-feet-get-it-your-damn-self type response. I would kill for that. Julie does anything I want. There's no challenge. I need that challenge."

I shook my head. I couldn't believe what he was saying. If I was into white women, Julie would have been the type of woman I would have wanted to be with. "Man, Julie has a great personality, she is intelligent, and she is damn attractive. Come on. Don't tell me you can't find a way to be head over heels for that."

Vic sat down on a stool by my miniature bar. "I can't, man. I can't do it anymore. Black women are my weakness. When I see a fine sister, I just get tingles, man."

I took a seat beside him. "Damn, Vic, I don't know what to say."

"Man, my skin is white, but you know me. What Colin is always saying is true—I am black on the inside; I love everything and anything about the black culture. It's all I know, man."

"I understand what you're saying, but when people look at you, they only see one thing."

"I know that."

"Damn, man. So what . . . you just don't think you can be with Julie like that? I mean, have you really thought about everything you're saying, what you're willing to give up?"

"Roy, I was thinking about it when I said, 'I do.'"

"So what are you going to do?"

"I don't know yet, man. That's why I'm telling you this. I need some advice, some real advice."

I drummed my fingers on the counter and exhaled. I didn't know what to say. On one level, I understood his desire to have the fire and attitude of a black woman because God knows I had that in Stacey. And that was one of the things I loved most about her. I could never have gotten her to do what Julie did with that beer. Stacey would've never gone for that. Honestly, it was a nice feeling to know that I could've never walked all over my wife like that.

But like everything, there was always a negative side. Stacey's black-woman-hear-me-roar attitude worked my last nerve sometimes, always complaining about something, always hollering about this or that. Shit, I wished she was passive sometimes, but then, like Vic, I knew I wasn't going to be happy.

"Man, I don't know what to tell you. This is something you are really going to have to sit and think about. I mean, you pledged your life to Julie. That's not easily overlooked."

"I know. And I've been thinking about it. But the more I do, the more I realize I will never truly be content. I've been holding this inside for a long time. I just can't anymore."

I continued to drum my fingers. Neither one of us said a word until Julie called his name to ask if he was ready to leave. Stacey would never have asked; she would have just told me she was ready.

Before going upstairs, I put out my hand. "Man,

I don't know if you fully realize what you're saying, but I got your back either way."

Vic looked at me with sad eyes. "Thanks, man. I needed to hear that."

Vic Reed

3

As Julie and I drove home, I couldn't help thinking about my conversation with Roy. I hadn't planned on talking about my desire to leave Julie, but when he started talking about how happy we should have been to be married, I felt like opening up to him. Besides, I needed someone to talk to, someone that I could rely on to give me some sound advice. And knowing that Colin would have only given all of the wrong advice, Roy was that perfect someone. He was always levelheaded about things and had a knack for making you look at things from another perspective. I needed to hear all of the positive things about Julie to realize that my staying in the relationship wouldn't be fair to her. She deserved unconditional love because that's what she was willing to give. After my talk with Roy, I knew that I had to leave.

I looked at my wife, who was sleeping peacefully, her head leaning against the window. *Damn, she is a beautiful and loving woman*. If I wanted to, I could be married to her until one of us passed away. She was the type of woman that my adoptive mother would have loved for me to marry. She was always saying, "Make sure you marry a girl that's gonna treat you right, Victor. Don't marry some tramp that ain't about nothin', ain't got nothin' to offer."

Well, Ma, although you passed before I married, Julie is definitely about something. She's college-educated, with a bachelor's degree in business. She's a successful real-estate agent. She knows how to cook and can't stand a dirty house. Someday she'll make a perfect mother. She's all that you would have wanted for me, Ma.

But she wasn't the one I wanted for myself.

I sighed as Julie stirred in her sleep. "Morning Dance" by Spyro Gyra played from the radio. I lowered the volume slightly. I didn't want to wake her. I just wanted to be alone with my thoughts. I had come to a crossroads in my life, and I had finally decided which way I wanted to turn. I should have felt bad about my decision, but instead I felt just the opposite. I felt like a weight had been lifted from my shoulders, a weight that had been placed there the day Julie announced to me that she was pregnant.

When we initially met, I had no real intention of us becoming a couple. My desire for black women was just too strong to really consider anything serious with Julie. Even though I had the blond hair and blue eyes, the sisters always knew I was down. Not having matured yet, I was really only interested in a physical relationship with Julie. I was a man, after all, and I would be lying if I said that her long, blond hair that went down to the middle of her back, mesmerizing eyes, and svelte figure didn't catch my attention. To my surprise, what started out as a couple of casual dates turned into a seven-month friendship. Never in a million years did I expect us to start dating seriously and that soon after she would get pregnant.

I remember the day she told me. I had actually been preparing myself to end things with her, because the desire to be with a black woman had been getting to me. Julie was a hell of a woman on both the inside and out, but I just couldn't deny the fact that as special as she was, I couldn't go on with her. But before I could drop my bomb, she dropped hers.

"Vic, I'm pregnant," she said.

I looked at her. "What?"

"I'm pregnant, Vic. I'm two months late with my period."

"How can you be so sure?"

"I took a pregnancy test and went to the doctor—both results were the same."

"But you're on the pill! You are on the pill, aren't you?"

"Of course I am! How could you ask me that?"

"How could you get pregnant?" I was pissed. Here I was getting ready to end the relationship and she comes with this shit.

"It's not like I tried to, Vic. You wanted to stop wearing a condom, remember?"

"Because you were on the pill!"

"And I was! And why are you yelling at me?"

"I'm not yelling!" I screamed.

Tears started flooding from her eyes. "Why are you mad at me, Vic? Don't you love me? Why aren't you happy about this?"

Damn, I hated to see a woman cry. That was like my kryptonite. I stepped to Julie and took her in my arms. Her tears cascaded down her cheeks and soaked my shoulder. "Don't cry, Julie," I said, forcing myself to speak softly. "Don't cry, okay?"

"Vic . . . I-I love you," she whimpered. "I don't want to lose you. I didn't mean for this to happen; I'll do whatever you want."

Do whatever I want? I thought.

"Do you want me to have an abortion?"

Aww, damn! Why did she have to go and ask me that? I held on tightly to her and bit down on my bottom lip. I knew how she felt about abortions. For her to ask me if I wanted her to have one was like handing me a rope to hang myself with. I was in a no-win situation. If I were to say yes, I would be an insensitive bastard; if I were to say no, then *she* would be happy and *I* would be miserable as hell. I wasn't ready to be a father, but I didn't like the idea of being a baby-killer either.

"No, Julie." I sighed. "I don't want you to do that. We'll figure something out."

"I love you, Vic."

I didn't say what I know she wanted to hear. I just held her in my arms.

Vic

4

For weeks, I stressed over Julie and her pregnancy. And to make matters worse, while I wanted to keep the whole situation a secret until I figured out what to do, Julie made it a point to tell her entire family and most of her friends. Things got ridiculous after that. I couldn't go a day without someone bringing up the *M* word. That's all I would hear—marriage, marriage, marriage; it frustrated the hell out of me.

I started having nightmares about it. I'd be in the middle of a courtyard, with a ball and chain wrapped around my ankles, while beautiful model-type sisters strolled around, prancing in their "thong-th-thong-thong-thongs," whistling at me. They all wanted me, and I damn sure wanted them. Although I tried, I couldn't move, but I was persistent. I tugged at the chain relentlessly, determined to break it and be set free. And just as the chain started to give way, a loud wailing noise would split the air.

As if on cue, all of the women would stand beside each other in a tight military line. Then Julie would step into the scene with a screaming baby in her arms. She'd have this evil grin on her face, reminiscent of the Joker's, and then she'd say, "You could have said yes to the abortion—I gave you an out; now you're mine for life."

I'd always wake up in a cold sweat after that. I just couldn't get away from the nightmare.

Finally, I broke down and told Colin and Roy about Julie's pregnancy and about the decision I'd made. We were playing pool at the Havana Club. "Fellas," I said above the loud salsa blaring from the speakers, "Julie's pregnant."

Roy and Colin froze in their tracks.

"What?" Colin asked. "She's pregnant?"

"Are you serious, man?" Roy questioned next.

I frowned. "Yeah, I'm serious. And I'm gonna marry her."

Colin put his stick down. "What do you mean, 'marry her'? You love her like that?"

I shrugged my shoulders and didn't answer for a second. Then finally I said, "I don't know, man."

Colin shook his head. "Well, if you don't know, how in the hell can you be talking about marrying her?"

"As much as I hate to admit it, Colin is right— you can't marry her if you don't love her," Roy said.

"Damn right, I'm right. Shit, just take her to get an abortion."

"Colin"—Roy looked at him with a sneer—"shut up."

"What?" Colin shrugged his shoulders. "He don't

want a baby, he don't know if he loves Julie . . . why *shouldn't* he consider an abortion?"

Roy slammed his hand on the pool table. "Man, that's the problem with you fools nowadays—get a girl pregnant and immediately brothers want to start talking abortion. Brothers don't want to step up and assume responsibility for their screw-ups."

"Why should he marry her and keep that kid if he ain't going to be happy?"

"Colin, I agree with you about him getting married, but I can't agree with you on the abortion. I mean, Stacey and I didn't plan on having Sheila and Jenea, but we assumed responsibility and haven't regretted it for one second."

"Yeah, but you guys had unconditional love; he don't know what he has."

"Which is why he shouldn't marry her. But he can take care of the kid."

"He don't want that kind of a headache, man. He can't have that kid, plain and simple."

As Colin and Roy went back and forth about me as if I wasn't there, I drank my beer in silence. Neither one of them knew how I really felt about being with Julie. I'd wanted to talk to Roy about my feelings, but I just never found the right time. And I knew I couldn't talk to Colin about it, because he would have just told me to keep Julie as my number one and have some fun on the side. I didn't want to do that. I was past the player stage in my life. Besides, Julie had done nothing wrong and didn't deserve to be disrespected like that. And now that she was pregnant, I didn't see how I could abandon her.

"Listen, fellas," I said, tired of being invisible, "both of you have made some valid points. Colin, you're right—I don't want the headache of fatherhood, but having the kid is not my decision to make. Even if I did have a say in it, abortion wouldn't be an option, because Julie is against that. Honestly, I don't really like the idea of killing my own child either."

"If you do it now," Colin said, "then you're not really killing anything."

"You're wrong," Roy stated.

I could tell that as a proud father, the talk of abortion disturbed Roy.

Roy added, "He would be killing something. As insignificant as it may seem to you, he would be killing a child, a child that could grow and change the world."

Colin sucked his teeth. He wasn't trying to hear any of what Roy had to say.

"Colin, Roy's right, man. I can't do the abortion thing. I morally could not do it."

"Thank you," Roy said.

"But as far as marriage goes, I know both of you are right about that. I shouldn't do it, but I have to, for the kid's sake. I don't want this kid being born out of wedlock. I went through life without knowing my real parents. And although I never went without love in my life, not knowing them was still a tough thing for me. I won't subject my child to the same thing."

"Vic," Colin said, "you don't have to marry the girl to be a parent."

"He's right about that, man," Roy agreed.

"I hear what you guys are saying, but I still have

to do it. I want my kid to have both parents always there, so that every day they will know they are loved and will never be alone. I don't want them having to split their time between homes—that's kind of like being an orphan, because there still is no real, permanent home. I won't allow that to happen. Now do me a favor and raise your beers and give your boy a toast. You two are going to be sharing best man honors."

As the recollection of that memory faded, I pulled the car into the driveway of our home.

Julie stirred and then opened her eyes. "Mmm . . . we're home already?"

"Yeah," I said softly, "we're home."

"I was dreaming. I had no idea I was so tired. Let's hurry inside so I can snuggle against you."

"Shit!"

"What is it?"

"I almost forgot that I have to go over a spreadsheet for work. I have a meeting tomorrow that I need to be ready for."

"Now? Honey, it's almost midnight."

I sighed and avoided her stare. "I know, but I really need to get this done. I put it off all weekend. I won't be too long, I promise."

Julie looked at me with a pout. I could see the disappointment in her eyes.

As she walked upstairs, I lowered my head and exhaled. As much as I wished I could, I couldn't change the way I felt. My head was never completely into the relationship, and since I knew that wasn't going to change, I moved out the next day.

Colin Ray

5

"**Y**eah, I know I haven't called, but I've been meaning to. Things have just been pretty hectic for me lately. No, I'm not lying, Tanecia! My boy split with his wife. He's been staying with me. I been dealing with his drama for the past two weeks. Damn, why you gonna get all loud and ignorant and shit? Yeah, I had a good time with you. I'm for real. I was gonna call you. Damn, can't we just be friends? Whatever." I hung up the phone and cursed out loud.

Vic looked up from his laptop. "What was that all about?"

I glowered at him. "Man, you are just fuckin' my whole shit up. Tanecia just called me a dog, man."

"You for real? *You* got called a dog?" Vic could barely hold back his laugh.

"Vic, that shit ain't funny! I have never ever been called that, as many freaks as I've been with. Man, you are just throwin' a wrench in my shit. Ever since you showed up at my spot, I have had absolutely no ass—none, zilch, zip, nada! Do you know how horny I am right now, dog? It's not like you would even help me out and come and chill and meet some females. All you wanna do is sit and mope. Man, what the hell for? You're the one who wanted to be out of your shit."

Vic's laugh subsided. "Man, I'm sorry. I know I put you in a bad way. I appreciate you letting me crash here. But for real, man, you go out and do your thing."

"Do my thing? Do my thing? Where? What? You think I'm gonna bring some ass here to let you hear me tap it? Bruh, please . . . my shows are for me and my cam only—no peeking or eavesdropping allowed."

"So go by them."

"Dog, it doesn't work that way. I do my shit here."

I picked up my book filled with phone numbers and grabbed a pen. "I can't believe I'm about to scratch a name from the book of fame." I furiously dragged a line through Tanecia's name and then threw the book on my leather sofa.

I'd always been good to go with the women. Mackin' ever since I was in high school, I showed my science teacher what chemistry was really all about. Mrs. Raymond—I would never forget her. She was fine as fine could get. She had every male in the school fiendin' for her—teachers and students alike. She would come to school dressed in form-fitting skirts and blouses with just enough buttons undone to reveal some cleavage. She was the original Halle Berry, only with braids and more ass. I had special "tutoring" sessions with her during my entire ninth grade year.

By the time the year was up, after not having done a single homework assignment, I passed with an A-plus average. I thought I was going to have summer sessions too, but her husband, who happened to be my algebra teacher, decided to spring a surprise vacation on her. He took her to the Florida Keys for a couple of months of R and R. When the next school year began, everyone but me was surprised when the police came to arrest her for having sex with a student. One of the faculty members caught her giving a senior a blowjob in the bathroom.

My luck didn't end after Mrs. Raymond; in fact my skills only improved. The fact that I was good-looking, with curly hair, bedroom eyes (so I've been told), and a killer smile always helped to make the game easy for me. I went from being a player amongst players to being the coach amongst coaches, schooling fools on the rules of the game.

By the time I hit my senior year, I'd already slept with most of the cheerleading squad, the field hockey team, and even a select few from the girls' basketball team. I was a legend by the time I graduated, and everyone loved me. If there was one thing my good-for-nothing father taught me, it was to always leave the woman smiling and never make her feel like she didn't matter. And that's what I did. That's why my book was so full that I needed to buy a new one.

* * *

"Twenty-nine years, man." I grabbed the remote for the TV. "Twenty-nine years and I have never had to lose a number."

Vic closed his laptop. "I said I was sorry, man."

I sucked my teeth and turned on the TV. I didn't say a word, instead I focused on the television. An old episode of *Sanford and Son* was on, helping to take the conversation with Tanecia off my mind. But as angry as I was about being called a dog, I was still glad to have Vic there.

We'd first met in junior high. We were in the same homeroom. Vic was a short, skinny nerd of a white boy who had no friends and no life. I don't know why I befriended him, as popular as I was. Maybe I felt sorry for him because he always wore hand-me-down clothes and lived in the projects, and had people picking on him about being adopted by a black woman who liked to beat his ass in broad daylight. Or maybe I just wanted to be a nice guy. Either way, I was glad I did, because we hit it off and became inseparable friends who backed each other through thick and thin. We went everywhere together, just hanging. As he helped me get my grades and priorities about school straight, I helped him develop his style. I never had to struggle too much to get him to be down. Before long, he was down like a brother, and as he got older and gained some muscle and confidence from the gym, he became a player like me. Together, we hit on every fine sister we could, leading the train at some of the most scandalous parties.

Vic was a Doberman to my Pit bull. And he didn't really calm down until he met Julie, which surprised the hell out of me, because I knew that he loved "blackberry queens." That's why it didn't surprise me much when he told me why he left her. But I had to be honest—I had come to like Julie. And the more I saw them together, the more I thought she was good for him, even if she wasn't a sister. She had all the qualities any man would want in a woman—intelligence, beauty, and a great personality—but obviously that wasn't enough for him.

"Man, you sure you want to end your marriage?" I asked while Fred Sanford held his chest and told his deceased wife, Elizabeth, he was coming to join her. "I mean, I know you weren't into the marriage thing in the beginning, but it seemed like it grew on you; I thought you were happy."

Vic leaned back on the sofa and kept his eyes glued to the television. "I'm sure. I've been thinking about this for a long time. I'm just not myself with Julie. I only stuck around so long because she needed the support after the miscarriage. She was in a bad way then; I couldn't leave her like that, you know."

"And you can leave now?" I tried to get him to look me in the eye, but he wasn't having it.

"I have no choice. My eyes keep wandering, and the temptation just keeps getting worse."

"Temptation's always going to be there, man. And it's always worse after you say 'I do.' "

"Yeah, I know, but it's hard to deal with it when you see its fine ass every day at work."

I looked at him from the corner of my eye. I shut off the TV.

"Hey, you know I like *Sanford and Son*," Vic said.

"Bunk that! What's up with this 'fine-assed temptation' you talkin' about? Don't hold out on a brother now that you've opened the can of worms."

Vic smiled and cracked his knuckles. "Maaan, there is this female at work—Latrice Meadows. Colin, she could make shit look good—she's that fine."

I shook my head. "You mean to tell me that you decided to leave Julie for her? Are you trippin'?"

"I didn't leave Julie for her; she was just the straw that broke the camel's back."

"What's so special about her . . . besides making shit look good?"

"Man, she just came to Intel a few months ago. She's a project engineer working the WorldCom account."

"Spare me the work details—I didn't ask about her resumé."

"A'ight, man. Anyway, she has an ass that won't quit; thick, shapely legs; breasts I want to nurse on until my stomach bursts; and best of all, she has the sweetest personality of any female I've ever known. We take breaks and lunches together sometimes and just talk. And when we're working, we send each other instant messages. She's real cool, man. And, as if you couldn't tell from the name, she's a sister."

"That's all well and good, man, but she doesn't sound that much different from Julie."

"She is way different from Julie, man. I mean, she has this whole attitude about her. It's like she could be a sweet angel one minute, and an angel with an attitude the next. She definitely has fire to her. Fire that I am just feeling every time I see her."

"So what . . . you gonna start dating her now?"

"Nah, man. We're just friends right now. I get looks here and there from her, but I'm still not sure if she has a thing for me."

"What does her body language say?"

"Can't tell yet; she's not an open book."

"Well, all I can say is, if you want it like you say you do, then you better make a playa move. Don't hesitate so that another dude can claim the prize before you do—that's always been my way of thinking."

"I have to do it slowly, man. I like her; I want to do it the right way. Besides, I have to move carefully because of this shit with Julie."

I nodded and turned the TV back on. I still couldn't believe he was for real about getting divorced. If I were him, I would've stayed with Julie and kept women "on the side for the rainy days," but not everyone was a true, bona fide player like me.

"Yo, have you spoken to Julie much these past couple weeks?"

"No. The way she screamed at me before I left, I figured it'd be better to let things cool off for a while."

"You sure she's not ready to talk now?"

"I doubt it. Besides, I don't want to face her right now. I don't want to see any more tears—that shit is tearing me up."

"Is it?"

Vic looked at me with a tight brow. "What do you mean by that?"

"Look, Vic, I'ma keep it straight with you—I hear what you're saying about not wanting to see Julie in any more tears, but I gotta be honest with you—it's almost hard to believe when you're sitting there talking about tryin' to get with some other female."

"Man, I don't like the fact that she's hurting. Believe me, if I could have done this any other way, I would have. And it really isn't so much that it's about Latrice. Like I said, she was just the straw. Colin, man, I've been unhappy for a while. Yeah, Julie is special, and yeah, I feel bad that she has to hurt, but I had to be happy. It was my turn."

"I feel you on that. I really do. And I'm not gonna front. It was big of you to do that, because if I were in your shoes, Julie would still be around and I would have the other chick too. But sooner or later, you're gonna have to face her again. And when you do, make sure you try to smooth things out with her, because she's a good person. Besides, it's better to get shit straight before all of the legal shit really starts. Try to make it a clean divorce."

"I hear you." Vic turned his attention back to the TV, which was now showing a re-run of the *Cosby Show*. I could tell that he didn't want to talk anymore, and neither did I, for that matter.

Talking about stress and drama was something I liked to avoid. I'd seen enough of it with my mom and dad to last me a lifetime. All of the arguments I had to listen to, all of the cursing and screaming—I swore growing up I wouldn't go through what they went through. And they weren't even

married! That's why I dedicated my life to bachelorhood and big pimpin'. No hassles, no worries,
no responsibility to anyone but myself—that's the
way I liked it.

Julie Reed

6

"I hate him!" I screamed, as another wave of tears fell from my eyes. "How could he do this to me, after all I've done for him, after everything that I've gone through? How could he be so damn selfish and insensitive? He's not in love with me? After all of the love I have shown him, he's not in love with me? Does that make sense?" I slammed my fist into the armrest of Stacey's sofa and squeezed my eyes tightly in the hopes that the tears would stop falling. They didn't. "No, it doesn't."

Stacey put her thick arm around me and let my head rest against her shoulder. She stroked my hair. "No, it doesn't, girl."

"I loved him unconditionally."

"I know you did."

I raised my head. "A divorce, Stacey? He wants a fucking divorce!" I stared at Stacey, who kept a tight lip and shrugged her shoulders. "For the past month, I have been sulking in my empty house, just trying to figure out why he's doing this, why he wants to end what we have, and do you know what I've come to realize?" I stood up. Tears continued to fall, although I was getting angrier. I blew my nose into an already-soaked tissue. "He doesn't want to be with me because I'm white!"

Stacey looked at me. "Julie, do you realize what you just said?"

I looked at her and curled my lips and crossed my arms. "I know exactly what I said."

"Julie, Vic is white. How could he not want you because you're white? Honestly . . . let's be serious."

"I *am* being serious. You know how Vic grew up. You see how he is. Stacey, Vic is more black than he is white; white is just his skin color. He loves black women, plain and simple."

"Julie, will you stop talking nonsense? Vic married you, not a black woman."

"And I'm sure he regrets every minute of it."

Stacey lifted my chin with her finger and looked at me through serious eyes. "Girl, listen, you need to stop this crazy talk, okay? Yes, Vic may have some nigga in him, but the last thing you need to do is to make yourself believe that he left you for a black woman. I mean, really, the world don't work that way. Besides, when it comes to the whole black-white issue, it usually works the other way around—black men are the ones crazy for the white meat." Stacey smiled.

From the look in her eyes, I could tell she was hoping I would crack one too, but I just couldn't, because in my heart, I knew what I was saying was true.

* * *

I could never ignore the fact that whenever we were out together and an attractive black female came around, his attention always seemed to drift in her direction. I tried to deny my feelings, though; I figured he was a man, and that's what men did. But I noticed that it was only the black women he paid attention to; that's why I stopped taking my pills—I wanted him to be *my* man.

He was dangerously handsome, with sparkling blue eyes and a smile warm enough to make your temperature rise by a few degrees. From the first moment I laid my eyes on him I was breathless. He stood out like no man I had ever met before. I found his pretty looks and bad-boy style intoxicating and was determined not to let him get away.

I was a little worried at first, when I told him about the pregnancy; I didn't know how he was going to take it. But as more time passed, I began to worry less. And after our wedding, I was sure that I had nothing to worry about.

When I had my miscarriage, I was heartbroken. I was looking forward to being a mother and was anxious to begin a family with him. The way he took care of me and stayed by my side through that ordeal only made my love for him stronger, so it was a real slap in the face when he told me he didn't want to be married anymore. I realized then that I had been wrong about everything.

I had been at home on the computer the night he told me. I was putting together a proposal for a house that I was going to be showing to a newlywed couple the next day. Vic had come in from work and went straight to the bedroom without saying a word to me. When I finished with my proposal, I shut off the PC and went into the bedroom to greet him.

I didn't know what to think when I saw him packing a suitcase. "Babe, what are you doing? Why are you packing?" I asked.

He didn't answer right away, nor did he even turn around.

"Earth to Vic . . . is something wrong? Why the silent treatment? You didn't even say hi when you came in. Did you have a bad day at work?"

He kept silent and continued to pack.

I was starting to get worried. "Vic, honey, what's wrong? Are you mad at me for something?"

He ignored me and continued to pack, going from one drawer to the next. Finally, after another couple of seconds, he turned around and looked at me. "Julie, I can't do this anymore." He moved to his dresser and started packing away his boxers and T-shirts.

In his eyes, I saw a darkness I had never seen. "Can't do what anymore?" I watched him closely. He didn't respond fast enough for me, so I asked again. "Vic, what are you talking about?"

Without looking at me, he said, "Julie, I'm moving out, and I want a divorce."

My heart stopped when he said that. Everything around me seemed to move in slow motion. "What do you mean, 'divorce'? Is this some kind of joke . . . because it's not a very funny one?"

"No joke." He finally turned to face me. "I don't want to be married anymore."

I got the chills, and my legs suddenly felt weak. I sat down on the edge of the bed and lowered my head. "Don't want to be married? What the hell are you talking about? What the hell are you trying to say?"

"I'm saying that I am not happy, I can't do this anymore. I love you, Julie, but I'm not in love with you. I'm sorry, but that's the way I feel." He turned back around and resumed packing.

I sat quietly and tried to absorb everything he'd just told me. I looked up at him, hoping to see him smiling. I only saw his back, and another suitcase being filled. I shook my head and bit down on my quivering lip. "Sorry? Vic, what do you mean 'not in love' with me? You married me, you exchanged vows with me! Not in love with me? Please tell me this is a sick, cruel joke you're playing. Please . . . This can't be happening. You can't mean what you just said. Vic? Vic! Please tell me the truth." I looked at him through pleading eyes, which were welling with tears.

He turned back around to face me.

I stood up and approached him slowly, grabbing him by the arm. I could tell by the wrinkle in his forehead that he was very serious, but I didn't want to believe it. "Vic, I love you. You love me too, remember?"

He pulled away from me slowly and zipped up both suitcases. "I'm sorry, Julie. I don't want to hurt you, but I can't go on with us anymore. Please forgive me. I'll be back for the rest of my things later. Goodbye." Without another word, he walked past me, bags in hand, and headed toward the front door.

I stood painfully still, not wanting to accept what was actually happening. I was still waiting for him to turn around and tell me it was all a lie, but when he opened the door, I knew that wasn't going to happen. "'Goodbye'? What the hell do you mean, 'goodbye'? You son of a bitch, why are you doing this? Is there someone else? Is that why you want to leave? Talk to me, you asshole! You married me."

Without turning around, he said, "I know, Julie. I'll have my lawyer contact you."

"'Lawyer'? Doesn't our marriage mean anything to you?" I stared at his back and held my breath.

"No," he said curtly and walked through the door.

My heart sank, and my tears fell in torrents down my cheeks. "You son of a bitch! You fuckin' son of a bitch, I hate you! I hate you! I hate you!"

"When he left, Stacey, I cried and blamed myself for everything. Even the miscarriage."

"Julie, that wasn't your fault, and you know it."

"I know, but I just couldn't understand why he would want to leave. Then I realized that it had never really been about love for him."

"What do you mean?"

"I mean, he has always had a thing for black women. Whenever we were out, I'd see his eyes wandering."

"All men do that."

"Yeah, but he never looked at white women."

"Come on, Julie."

"No, it's true, Stacey. But it wasn't just the stares. Whenever we went out and we were around black women, he always treated me differently—he was colder to me, less sensitive. There were times when I just felt like he was completely uncomfortable with me by his side."

"I don't know, Julie. The idea of him being uncomfortable is a little far-fetched; maybe if he were black, I could see it."

"Stacey, he practically is. I'm telling you, that's what it is—he couldn't deal with my color."

"Julie, I don't know . . . I just find that hard to believe."

"Oh, believe it, Stacey. I've known it for a long time, but I tried to ignore what I saw. I tried to lie to myself and think our relationship would last—it's the only thing that makes sense to me."

"I know you may not want to hear this, but isn't it possible that he just fell out of love with you? It happens; I've been through it."

"I know it happens, but not in this case. I'm not wrong about this." I sat down on the sofa and thought about the things I had said. I knew I was right. Even though I tried to deny it, for as long as I'd been with Vic, I'd always felt like the runner-up in a beauty contest and was just now admitting it to myself.

Stacey Burges

7

"I saw Julie today," I said, handing Roy his plate of food. I took my own food out and sat down across from him. I had already fed Sheila and Jenea and gotten them off to bed.

Roy took a bite of the baked chicken I made and then took a sip of his beer.

I had been waiting all day to have a moment with just the two of us. Julie's visit had been on my mind all day.

"Really?" He let out a small burp. "What did she want?"

"To talk. She's pretty torn up over what's going on with her and Vic. I have to admit, I'm pretty shocked myself; I never thought they would be going through anything like this. Julie was in tears practically the whole time." I swallowed a mouthful of food and drank some of my juice. I had outdone myself with the chicken. It was good.

"Yeah, I can imagine," Roy said, inhaling the food.

"She's taking Vic's decision to end their marriage really hard. She's got this crazy notion that the reason he wants out is because she's white—can you believe that? I tried to convince her that there had to be another reason, but she was pretty adamant about her feelings. Julie's my girl and all, but that is crazy, wouldn't you agree?"

Roy swallowed the last of his chicken and gulped down the rest of his beer. If there was one thing I could always count on, it was his hearty appetite. Looking at me, he said very quietly, "She's right."

"Excuse me?"

"Vic told me about what he was going to do a couple of weeks ago. And he told me why."

"Wait a minute—you mean to tell me that you knew he was going to leave her and you didn't say a word to me? And what do you mean, 'she's right'? Are you saying he really wants out because she's white?"

"That's what I'm saying. And I didn't say anything because I know you and Julie are close, and I figured it was best to keep quiet about it; I didn't want to be in the middle of anything."

"So what, you don't think I can keep quiet about something like that? You trying to say I have a big mouth?" I looked at him, crossed my arms, and curled my lips. I couldn't believe he knew and hadn't confided in me.

"Stacey, what would you have done if I told you Vic didn't want to be with Julie anymore?"

"I would have told Julie."

"Exactly. So to answer your question—yes, you do have a big mouth."

"How could you expect me not to say anything, Roy? Julie is my friend. You think I like seeing her go through this? I mean, this is ridiculous—her heart is broken because he wants a black woman?—what kind of bullshit is that? And if that's the case, then his ass should have realized that before he ever married her. This is the stupidest thing. Vic is as white as Julie is!"

"Baby, I know."

"So why did he ask her to marry him?"

"He felt he had no choice."

"No choice?"

"He was planning on ending their relationship, but the night he was going to tell her, she told him she was pregnant. He felt like he couldn't end it then."

"Why? That doesn't make sense. What—he didn't think she could handle it without him?"

"No, that's not it. And it does make sense. Remember, a black woman raised Vic. He never knew his mother or father. He swore to himself that he wouldn't let his child grow up like that."

"Okay. But why propose?"

"He didn't want the child to have to be split between two homes. He was trying to do the right thing, but he wasn't happy. He loved her, but he was never *in love* with her."

"So I bet he was relieved when she had the miscarriage, huh?—just like a man."

"No. Actually, he was looking forward to being a father. When it happened, he was hurt over it. And, believe it or not, he was worried about Julie, which is why he didn't leave right away. But now that time has passed, he's come to a point where he just can't live a lie anymore."

I slammed my hand down on the table. "That is pure *BS*. I'm sorry that your white boy has a thing for black women, but the fact remains, he said, 'I do.' You can't just change your mind and say, 'I don't'!—that is so cowardly."

"Look, don't yell at me about it. I didn't tell him to leave her. I even tried to talk some sense into him. I told him how great Julie is, and how lucky he was to have her, but his mind was made up a long time ago. He said he wants the fire and attitude a black woman has."

"'Fire and attitude'? What does he want—a ghetto bitch?"

Roy shrugged his shoulders. "I don't know. All I know is he's not happy."

"So because she takes care of him and doesn't give him attitude, he's not happy? Does he realize how ridiculously stupid that sounds? I can't believe this." I stood up and grabbed Roy's empty plate and my own, which was still filled with food. I had lost my appetite.

Julie was a beautiful, intelligent, kind human being. I liked her from the first moment I met her. She didn't deserve any of what Vic was doing to her.

"All because of her skin color? Is Vic really that naïve? Julie is special. She doesn't have one mean or ignorant bone in her body—is that not good enough for him? I mean, does he really think he will find greater happiness with a black woman? Does he not realize that we can be bitches when we want to be too?"

"Stacey, yelling at me is not going to do you or Julie any good. I hear what you're saying, but his mind is made up."

"Well, then change his mind! Julie is too beautiful a person for him to do this to her. Shit, you men walk around and complain about not being able to find a good woman, and then when you do, you either dog her out like that egotistical, too-damned-high-on-himself Colin, or you say, 'She's not good enough,' like that fool Vic—y'all make me sick!"

"Stacey, again, you're yelling at the wrong person. I know I have a good thing; you don't see me complaining."

"And you better not either. I swear if you even try to be like Colin, or that idiot Vic, I will squeeze your balls until your eyes bulge."

Roy laughed, not realizing how serious I was.

I definitely had the fire and attitude, and I never made empty threats. I walked out of the kitchen and went into the living room. I was fuming, and I knew I was taking it out on the wrong person. But I couldn't help it; he was there.

I popped the *Waiting to Exhale* DVD in, and forwarded to the scene where Angela Basset burned her cheating husband's clothing in his car. As the scene played, I thought, *Julie should have done that to Vic's ass.*

Roy walked into the living room when the fire was ablaze. When he saw what I was watching, he made an immediate beeline for the bedroom. He knew to leave me alone at that moment.

I watched the scene two more times and then turned off the TV.

When I walked into the room, Roy was in bed watching ESPN. I looked at him and said, "Julie is my friend and will always be my friend. *She* will be coming over here—I don't want Vic here anymore."

He looked at me with surprise.

I didn't care. And I was serious. "Look, if Vic wants to be an asshole, then let him be one. But Julie is my girl—I don't want Vic's immature ass over here."

"Hold up, Stacey. I understand Julie is your girl, but Vic is my boy. Their problems are their problems, not mine—I suggest you adopt the same philosophy."

"So what . . . you're choosing his side over mine?"

"Baby, it's not about sides; they are our friends. Because they're going through something, that doesn't mean that our friendships have to change. Now, I didn't tell you I didn't want Julie here—"

"—Because you know she didn't do anything!" I yelled louder than I intended.

"Will you keep your voice down? You're going to wake the girls. Look, there is no real right and wrong here. You can't fault Vic because he is not in love with Julie; he has every right to feel that way."

"Well, his sorry ass should have never married her. He's only doing her more harm. And I don't care, Roy—I don't want him here. He is not welcomed in this house."

"In which house? You said 'this house,' but you're obviously not talking about *our* house."

"Hell yes, I meant here—I don't want to see him."

"Well, then you can leave when he comes over. Vic is my boy, like Julie is your girl—that's not going to change, and my friendship with him won't change."

"Roy, I swear I don't want him here." I stared hard at my husband. I couldn't believe he was taking the stance he was. I couldn't believe he was choosing sides like that.

"I pay the bills here just like you do, Stacey. As a matter of fact, I pay the majority of the bills here, so I don't care about what you want or don't want. Vic is coming over, and that's final."

"Oh no, you didn't. You didn't just go there with me and the bills, did you? I don't see your ass taking care of our little girls every single hour of every single day. I don't see you cooking and cleaning and running this household. Don't you even try to cheapen my worth to this house."

"Baby, that's not what I meant—"

"Don't you 'baby' me, Roy. I said I don't want Vic here, and *that* is final." I stormed out of the room before he could say another word, and before our argument got any worse. Cursing the whole way there, I went to the living room, turned on the TV, and this time I watched the entire movie even angrier than before. Vic's decision had brought to surface some deeply buried feelings.

Vic

8

I finally worked up the nerve to ask Latrice out on a date, something I had been debating for the past few weeks. I remember when I first saw her. It was in the break room. I was getting my morning coffee and toasting a bagel when she walked in. I was like a cartoon character whose tongue had fallen out and rolled open like a red carpet—she was that fine. She had a thick but well-proportioned, hourglass figure and didn't attempt to hide her thick, shapely legs in the black mini-skirt she was wearing. To go with the skirt, she wore a light-blue, V-neck blouse, and even though it wasn't the tightest of tight, her breasts could still be seen swelling beneath the fabric. She was all woman.

I tried my best to be discreet as I watched the sashay of her ample behind while she moved to the refrigerator and put her lunch bag inside. I was focusing on her so hard that had she not alerted me, I could have set the building on fire.

"Your toast is burning." She smiled.

I turned toward the toaster and saw the smoke. "Oh shit!" I moved to it and popped the bread, which had burned and was flaking.

With a laugh, Latrice said, "I guess you should have been keeping your eyes on that toast." Without saying another word, she left the break room, leaving me alone with my mess and my embarrassment.

Since that day, I did what I could to find out about her. Through some slick investigation, thanks in large part to my friend, Al, from the mailroom who can get info better than the CIA, I found out Latrice had just recently started with Intel's Project Engineering group. Al also informed me that she worked out at the gym religiously, had her own condo, no kids, and more importantly, no man. But of course, one major problem still remained—I was married. So, for a while, I had to be content with making small talk with her whenever I could; we'd say 'hi' and have small conversations about the job, nothing too heavy.

We eventually started trading e-mails back and forth, talking via the instant messenger whenever we weren't too busy. When our schedules permitted, we'd meet for lunch. Latrice was cool and down-to-earth. She also had a regal attitude about her, like she knew she was the shit. That was definitely drawing me in. The more we talked, the more I wanted to get to know her. And because of my growing desire for her, I had to make the decision to finally end the marriage with Julie.

But it wasn't really just Latrice who led me to that decision. The fact of the matter was, if Latrice didn't come into the picture, it would have been someone else eventually, because I wasn't satisfied at home.

Telling Julie wasn't an easy thing for me to do, but it was necessary. For so long, I had been living my life for her, trying to make her happy because she was pregnant. Then when she lost the baby, I spent my time trying to cheer her up. But enough was enough. I wanted to live my life and be happy for me—that's why I did what I did, and that's why I finally asked Latrice out.

The workday had ended, and I was tying up some loose ends before leaving. I also waited because I didn't want anyone else around when I stepped to Latrice. I was nervous, and I wasn't sure how she was going to respond to my advance. I locked my office up and went down to the other end of the building, where she was sitting in her office in front of her PC.

I knocked on the door. "Hey, you," I said.

Latrice looked up and smiled. Damn, her smile was intoxicating.

"Hey, Vic! What's up? I'm surprised you're still here," she replied.

"Yeah," I said, taking a seat. "I had some things to take care of. I have another all-day meeting."

"Don't you just love those?" Latrice asked sarcastically.

"Oh, yeah—about as much as I love migraines—which I always seem to get when I walk out of those."

Latrice laughed then looked at her watch. "Damn!"

"What's up?"

"I forgot I was supposed to meet my girl, Emily, at the gym at seven-thirty tonight. She couldn't go at our normal time, so we had to go late."

"You go every night?"

"Like clockwork."

"That's cool. I go at least four days a week."

"What gym do you go to?"

"Supreme Sports Club. You?"

"Emily and I go to Bally's over in Ellicott City."

"I've been there a few times. It's cool. Has some nice-looking women."

"Just like a man—I thought you went to work out."

"I do," I said with an innocent smile. "My eyes are burned out after each set."

"Mmm hmm. I bet." Latrice started to shut down her PC.

My heart started beating heavily. This would be the first time I had asked anyone out since I started dating Julie. I was hoping the rust wouldn't show. "Hey, Latrice, there was something I wanted to ask you."

Locking her drawers, she said, "What's up?"

"Well, you know how we've been taking lunch breaks sometimes, and chatting on IMessage or e-mail?"

"Yeah. It's been fun. You're one of the few people I can stand here at Intel—consider yourself lucky."

I smiled. "Oh, I do. And it has been fun. Which is why I was wondering if you'd consider hanging outside of the office one night? Maybe just chill and take in a movie or some dinner."

Latrice stopped what she was doing and looked at me.

I felt my throat get dry. The look on her face was hard to read. I wondered if I had crossed the boundary lines of the friendship we had established. But then shit! I had to do that to keep from falling into the doomed "just-a-friend" pit. I didn't pull my eyes away; I wanted her to know I was serious.

An uncomfortable fifteen seconds passed. "Vic, aren't you married?" she asked with an edgy tone that I'd never heard her use before—at least not with me.

"Technically, yes, but we're getting a divorce."

"Don't tell me you're divorcing your wife to ask me out." She lightened her tone just a little.

"No, no. Our relationship was over long before you and I met."

"Uh huh. Vic, why you wanna take me out?"

"You're cool, Latrice. I'd like to be able to completely kick back and relax with you away from the stiffs here. I mean, if you're not comfortable with it, that's okay. I'd understand. I'm not trying to upset you." I watched her and held my breath. I couldn't figure out how she was taking the invite.

She stood up, slipped into her coat, and grabbed her laptop case.

Following her cue, I stepped out of her office.

She locked her door. "A divorce, huh? Let me think about it and get back to you." Without saying goodbye, she walked away, leaving me there to wonder what her answer would be.

Latrice

9

"I have a problem, girl," I said, approaching my forty-fifth minute on the Stairmaster.

Emily, who was on her thirtieth, huffed. "What's up?"

"Girl, you remember me telling you about my friend at work, the one I take lunch breaks with sometimes?"

"The white guy with the cute smile and the pretty eyes?"

"Yeah." I wiped beads of sweat from my forehead and increased the speed of motion. "That's him."

"What about him?"

"Girl, you would not believe what happened before I came here. Girl, *I* can't believe what happened."

Emily looked at me. Sweat fell from her chin. "What?"

I got off the Stairmaster. "We need to talk, girl. Let's go get our things and get out of here." As we got our bags from the locker room, I told her all about Vic's invitation.

"Are you for real? He asked you out?"

"What do you mean, he asked me out? You think I'm not fine enough to be asked out? Why would I make that up?"

Emily shook her head and laughed. "You know I didn't mean it like that, so don't even trip. I'm just surprised, that's all. Didn't you say that he was married?"

"Yeah, but he says he's getting a divorce."

"I see. But he's *white*."

"Girl, he is blacker than some of the darkest brothers at my job."

"But he's still white."

"So are you."

"We're not talking about me, though, Trice; we're talking about you. And if I recall correctly, I remember hearing you say more than once that you do the right thing by not doing the white thing. Am I wrong?"

I shook my head and sucked my teeth. "Yeah, I said that."

White men with black women had always been taboo for me—even more so than a black man and a white woman. Plus, white men were so hypocritical when it came to their attraction for black women. Unlike the brothers, who had no qualms about flaunting the "prize" on their arm, white men always kept their feelings for a sister on the down low. Oh, they had no problem hitting the ass behind closed doors, but when showtime came, it was like all of a sudden black women weren't good enough to be with.

"So what did you tell him? I hope you weren't too hard on him. From the way you talk about him, he seems like a nice guy."

"Yeah, Vic is nice. Real nice."

"You going to be able to keep your friendship with him? I mean, does he seem like he could handle the rejection?"

I didn't answer her as we walked to our cars.

"'Trice? You're not answering me. You did say no, didn't you?"

I avoided her stare as I reached in my purse to grab my car keys.

"Trice!"

"Okay, okay. Damn! No, I didn't turn him down, and no, I didn't say yes; I told him I would get back to him."

"You what? Oh no! Don't tell me you've got 'jungle fever.'" Emily clapped her hands and started laughing.

I shook my head. "Em, stop trippin'. All I said was that I'd get back to him. And let's not go there, Miss 'Fever Queen.'"

"Hey, at least I admit it. So you're serious about getting back to him?"

I shrugged my shoulders. "Girl, I don't know."

"Latrice and a white man—who would have thought it?"

"I didn't say yes yet! Besides, I already told you he's more black than OJ."

"OJ's black?"

"Sheeeit—don't get me started on that fool. Anyway, like I was saying, Vic has a lot of soul. I mean at work, he plays the game well, but when it's the two of us trippin', he lets his true self out."

"Which is?"

"Let me put it this way—he was raised by a black woman in the projects in DC."

"Really? A black woman?"

"He was adopted."

"Oh. So now back to my original question, which you never really answered—you serious about getting back to him?"

"I told you I don't know."

"If you don't know, that means you're giving it some thought. And if you're giving it some thought, that means that you have the fever for the flavor. So don't even try to deny that." Emily raised an eyebrow and straightened her lips.

Damn. "Okay. Yeah, I may be feeling him a little."

"I knew it!" Emily screamed.

"Girl, keep your voice down."

"Latrice is feeling the white boy, Latrice is feeling the white boy . . ."

"Em"—I shot her a look.

"Okay, okay—white-black-boy. So, Miss 'I'll-never-date-a-white-man-because-he-just-don't-do-any-thing-for-me,' what is it about him that you like?"

"Girl, I don't know. There's just something about him. He's so down-to-earth and cool. I can actually trip with him. I mean his skin may be white, but he's so damn real. Maybe that's why the skin color doesn't bother me too much . . . I don't know."

"And his being married—what's up with that?"

"I told you, 'he says he's getting a divorce.'"

"He still wearing the ring?"

"No. I checked for that."

"Still doesn't mean he couldn't be lying about

that, you know how men are. You know how Jeff was—a dog, if there ever was one."

"Yeah, I know," I said softly.

The mention of Jeff, Emily's former boss and an all-around dog, took my thoughts to my best friend, Danita Evans. She used to mess around with Jeff, who was also her boss. She lost her man Stephen, who I still spoke to every now and then, over Jeff's triflin' ass. Danita died in a car accident two years ago, the same night Stephen got married to another woman. Her death hit me hard. Danita was like my sister, only closer. We were on the outs for a while because I couldn't support what she had going on with Jeff. Plus, I liked Stephen. He didn't deserve what Danita had been doing. But after he left and moved on with his life, Danita swallowed her pride and apologized to me for what she did, and our friendship continued as if it had never stopped.

The night that Danita died, everything changed. I was in a state of depression for months. I couldn't sleep or eat—which was a tremendous thing, as much as I enjoyed food.

To make matters worse, my relationship with my then boyfriend, Bernard, began to suffer. It wasn't really his fault. All he wanted was a little love from me, but I found it difficult to give. As much as I loved him and wanted to be with him, Danita's death wouldn't allow me to be happy. As I sank deeper and deeper into my pit, Bernard started to drift away from me. And because I never tried to reel him in, he drifted into the arms of another woman—that was another bitter pill for me to swallow.

Over time, and not by my choice, I began to lose all of the weight I had amassed over the years. One rainy day, I caught my reflection in the mirror as I stepped out of the shower. I had to admit, I looked good. I had lost so much weight, I almost didn't recognize myself.

That same day, I called Emily, who had since become my best friend, and told her I wanted a partner to join the gym. We joined together, and since then I'd lost more than one hundred pounds and had become a health nut. Instead of McDonald's and Kentucky Fried, I started eating nothing but salads and low-fat, low-carb foods. I became a serious calorie-counter. And I was glad I did.

As I lost weight, my self-esteem improved; my stamina increased, which was a plus in the bedroom, and the extremely fine men who used to ignore me started taking second glances. Of course, I'd always had men salivating over my ghetto booty, which I still had, but as the weight disappeared, they drooled over the whole package, and not just a slice.

With every day that passed, I became happier and more intent on becoming a new person. Eventually I made the switch from E-Systems Communications to Intel, Inc. Through a hook-up from a former manager of mine, I got a position as a project engineer.

It was during my first week there that I met Vic. I can't lie—when I first met him I thought he was attractive . . . even for a white guy. He had a smile that was too pretty, innocent eyes, and a physique that told me he wasn't a slouch. I had seen him in passing a few times, but he never really noticed me—not until he burned his toast checking me out in the break room. I walked in to put my lunch in the refrigerator while he was there getting his breakfast together. I could feel his eyes on me as I went about my business, and I made sure to take my time doing it. Since dropping the weight, I'd made it a point to enjoy the admiration men had for me.

Unfortunately, I had to break the spell when I saw the smoke coming from the toaster. As Vic blushed and went to take care of his food, I caught the wedding band on his finger. After that, whatever thoughts may have been creeping into my mind quickly went away. I wasn't trying to get caught up like Danita; I had too much respect for myself to become a trick on the side—besides, he was white. But that didn't stop me from becoming friends with him. We'd stop and have small talk in the hallway sometimes. We'd pass by each other's office just to say hi.

Eventually, we spoke back and forth over e-mail and the Instant Messenger. The more we talked and got to know each other, the more I started to feel him. He caught me by surprise when he asked me out. Never one to talk about his personal life, I had no idea that he and his wife were having problems. But when he told me about getting a divorce, and I saw that his ring wasn't on his finger, I shocked myself by saying I would think about it.

"Girl, I don't think he'd lie. I know men will be men, and boys will be boys, but Vic's different.

And as amazing as this sounds coming from me, the color don't mean a thing."

Emily leaned against her Chrysler Sebring and stared at me with an open mouth. Then she put on a fake crying act. "My girl is growing up!" She laughed.

"Oh whatever." I rolled my eyes at her. "I'm already grown; I'm just willing to expand my horizons this one time . . . maybe."

"One time, huh? Well, you know, girl, once you go white—"

I put my hand up and cut her off immediately. "Don't you even go there."

Emily's face turned beet-red from laughing. "So you're really going to consider it, huh?" she asked, composing herself.

"Maybe. I mean, I have to think of the consequences. You know I have my rep to keep up. I'm not trying to damage that. Plus, there's that whole inter-office, interracial relationship thing to think about."

"'Relationship'? Damn! All the man asked for was a date."

"You know how I think ahead. But anyway, I also have to make sure that he is for real about the divorce, because I am not trying to get caught up in no drama—I don't want to have to come out my face and kick some ass."

"True. So when are you going to answer him?"

"Don't know. I'll let him wait while I analyze everything. Then I'll tell him my answer."

"Okay, girl." Emily got into her car. "Just make sure you let me know."

"You know I will."

Emily smiled, and as she drove off, she started singing again. *You've got jungle fever . . .*

I smiled and shook my head. "You're one to talk, girl. You ain't ever felt anything but the fever."

As I drove home, I thought about when I would tell Vic yes.

Vic

10

"**F**ellas, Latrice said yes," I declared, as I claimed my first victory for the night. We were at Havana Club for our weekly Wednesday night pool session, something we'd been doing since Colin first suggested it three years ago. After that first night, we'd been hooked. We also got a chance to enjoy the salsa music, check out the women, and have an occasional cigar, and the wives never knew.

"'Yes' to what?" Roy racked the balls. It was his turn for a beating.

"Do you always forget what we talk about, man?" Colin sipped on his beer as he checked out a fine Latin sister shaking her bon-bon on the dance floor. "Latrice is the honey from his job he been sweatin'. He's been talking our ears off about her."

"Oh, yeah—my bad," Roy said.

"You getting forgetful in your old age, dog?" Colin smiled.

"Man, I got two kids and a wife. Vic's love life is the last thing on my mind." Roy turned his attention back to me. "So you finally worked up the nerve, huh?"

I didn't answer him right away. I was concentrating on my break to begin our game.

Pool was something I enjoyed playing. I'd been doing it since I was a teenager. When things were hectic outside in the projects, I knew better than to be a knucklehead. I'd escape to some of the pool halls, where the owners were kind enough to let me in to chill with the big boys. I learned the art of pool by getting my behind beaten. Soon enough, *I* started doing the ass whupping.

After breaking the rack and sinking the nine and three balls, I said, "Yeah, man. I figured the time was right."

"She knows you're getting divorced, right?" Roy asked.

"Yeah. I told her."

"Speaking of which," Colin said, "what's up with that, anyway?"

"Man, it's rougher than I thought it would be."

Colin asked, "Julie still not speaking to you?"

"Yup."

"Be glad she's not," Roy said. "She's been by my place a couple of times, and I hear her and Julie talking."

"Yeah, what's she saying?" I asked.

"Man, you don't even want to know."

"Damn!" I said softly.

"Yeah, 'damn' is right. Man, when she and Stacey get together . . . well, I'll just put it like this—sometimes I'm afraid for my life. They give me looks like they want to do something evil. Let me just warn you ahead of time—when you come over on Sunday to watch the game, be ready for a very, very cold reception."

Colin pulled his gaze away from the dance floor and looked at Roy. "Damn, dog, your wife is hatin' like that?"

"Oh, she's past hate, man. Vic is in the infamous coward-ass-man category."

"Damn!" Colin laughed. "When Stacey puts you in that category, there ain't no comin' out."

I sank another ball and took a sip of my Coors. "I expected that to happen, fellas. Stacey and Julie are tight. I knew Julie would be talking to her, and I knew Stacey would have anger toward me—that's what women do. I can't blame Julie or Stacey for being mad, but shit, it's better that I bailed out than mess around."

"I beg to differ," Colin said.

Roy finally prepared to take a shot after I narrowly missed sinking the eight ball, having left all of his balls on the table. "Colin, your opinion doesn't count."

"Yeah," I added. "Man, even if you had the finest honey in the world, you would still play her."

"Hey, y'all know I can't stand a one-course meal— I gotta have appetizers and desserts," Colin said.

"Yeah, okay." Roy missed his next shot, and I went on to claim my second victory off a nice bank shot.

As Colin racked for his beating, I looked at Roy. "So Stacey is really feeling bitter, huh? What did you tell her?"

"Nothing that she didn't already hear from Julie.

I tried to explain why you couldn't go on, and how it was better that you were honest than to be like Colin."

"He's not that lucky," Colin interjected.

I ignored Colin. "What did she say?"

"Man, she nearly bit my head off. She couldn't understand how you could not want Julie because of her color."

"It's more than that, and you know it."

"I know. And I tried to tell her that, but it didn't make a difference. She thinks you're a coward, plain and simple."

"Man, I'm doing the right thing."

"Never in a woman's eyes," Colin said. "We can never do the right thing—that's why I avoid the shackles."

"Oh, and get this"—Roy downed his beer— "Stacey doesn't want you coming to the house."

Colin looked at me. "Dayum! She's hatin' on your ass for real." He all but fell over laughing.

"Don't worry, though, she can chew me out and scream all she wants—it's my house too."

I shook my head. "Damn, man, I can't believe she's giving you grief like that over this."

"Of course, she is! That's what women do. You two probably argue at least three nights a week over Vic and Julie, don't you?" Colin laughed.

"Man, try four. She's pissed because I still hang out with you and won't agree to not let you come over. She's gone to some extreme level, and I don't understand why."

"Women!" Colin declared. "When one of them cries over a man, no matter what he did or didn't do, they form some kind of man-hating alliance, where the objective is to give hell to every other male they can. Damn, maybe I can afford to miss the game this week."

I shook my head. "Damn, man. I'm sorry you have to feel the effects of this."

"Man, it's cool. I can deal with my wife."

"Oh yeah." Colin prepared to take a shot. "Just wait until she stops givin' up the ass—you know that's gonna happen next, right?"

"No way," Roy said.

Colin sank a six-nine combination. "Give it about another week, and you'll be in the same category with Vic. Shit, you might even be sleeping on the couch."

"Never in my house, man. Besides, Stacey wouldn't do that."

"Vic"—Colin looked at me—"I have fifty bucks that says his ass is on the couch after Sunday."

I looked at Roy and sighed. "I'm not gonna bet on that one."

"Yeah, because you know I'm right." Colin sank another combo and then went on to kick my behind—royally.

By that time, my head was out of the game. After we played another two games, and after Colin collected a waitress' number, we all went our separate ways.

I had finally gotten a new condo two weeks earlier and was settled in. Sitting on my couch, I thought about the changes in my life. I really did care for Julie, and I never intended on hurting her. Some nights, the regret for letting things between us go as far as they did hit me hard. I'd come across so many women who'd been done wrong or who'd had their hearts broken; I never thought I would actually be one of those men that they cried and complained about. I actually took some pride in the fact that I had never let a relationship end in a negative way. To this day, I was still cool with every woman I'd messed with. Julie was my first heartbreak, and hopefully my last, because knowing that I caused her tears to fall made me feel terrible. That's why I neglected her calls and avoided talking to her—I just couldn't deal with the guilt I felt. And even though I knew that leaving was the right decision, I still couldn't help feeling like I was in the wrong. I mean, let's face it, Julie may not have been perfect, but she did her best to show me nothing but love. And like Roy said, there was no denying her worth. So even if I'd tried not to, how could I not feel guilty for hurting her? But as bad as I felt, I couldn't deny the fact that I was happier. I didn't feel the same type of pressure that I felt before. I was free to be myself and not have to put on an act for anybody. I just hoped things with Latrice would go smoothly.

I was in my office getting ready to go when she said yes. It had been a little over a week and a half since I'd first asked her out. During that time, I noticed how she distanced herself from me. Our e-mail and IM exchanges decreased, and we'd only had lunch together twice. Although I was dying to know her answer, I never asked her what her decision was—I didn't want her to think I was pressed. Besides, I figured if she didn't want to go out with me, I at least wanted us to remain friends.

But with each day that passed, I was losing more and more hope about even that possibility. So when she came by and said, "So when and what time are you pickin' me up?" I was surprised.

I looked at her for a long couple of seconds. "What was that?" I asked.

She put her hands on her hips and tilted her head to the side, her feline eyes slit just a fraction. "I know you didn't forget about asking me out."

I smiled on the outside and screamed *Hallelujah* on the inside. "Oh," I said, keeping my cool. "That's right. I did ask you out—about a year ago."

"Oh, you got jokes." She stepped into the office and closed the door.

"Every now and then."

"Well, okay, Mr. Funnyman—when and what time?"

"Does that mean your answer is yes?"

"You know, I can leave now." She turned toward the door.

Quickly, I said, "Seven-thirty on Friday. Denzel's movie starts at ten. I figured we could do dinner before then."

"Oh, how you know I wanna see a movie?"

"I heard you talking about it with your friend on the phone."

Latrice smiled an innocent smile. She asked in a high-pitched Steve Urkel-like whine, "Did I do that?"

I laughed and shook my head. "So now *you*'ve got the jokes."

"Oh, I have 'nuff jokes."

"So seven-thirty on Friday is cool?"

"Yeah. But before we set this in stone, I need to ask you something."

"Shoot."

"Why'd you ask me out?"

"'Why?'"

"Did I stutter?—and don't answer my question with a question."

I nodded slowly. "Because I wanted to hang out with you outside of work," I said honestly. I left out that she was fine and I wanted to get to know her on a more intimate level.

"I've never dated a white guy before." She stared at me seriously. "Not once; I've never even come close."

"I guess I'm lucky."

"Mmm hmm. I'm not really attracted to white men—they usually don't stimulate me."

I was enjoying her candor. "And I do?"

"Let's just say, you're not as dull as the rest of them."

"Let's just."

"So tell me—do you like all women, or does my skin color fascinate you?"

"First of all, I love all women. And second, if you're asking me if I asked you out because I was curious, the answer is no. You wouldn't be the first black woman I've ever gone out with."

"I see. And you just want to hang out outside of work, huh?"

"That's right. But let me ask you something— why did you say yes?"

Latrice licked her lips and passed her hand

through her braided hair. "Did you want me to say no?"

I shook my head. "You know the answer to that—and don't answer my question with a question."

"Humph," she said with another smile.

"Was it my color that you were curious about?"

"No." She stepped toward me. "Like I said, you're not as dull as the rest of them. And you're kind of cute."

"'Kind of'?"

"Kind of."

I laughed. "Well, you're kind of cute too."

Latrice sucked her teeth. "Please . . . I know you like what you see."

Neither one of us could hold back our laughter.

Latrice removed a card from her purse and handed it to me. "My cell number is on there. Call me for directions." She turned around and opened the door.

"Just for directions?"

She looked at me over her shoulder. "You have the number." Conversation over, she walked out, leaving me alone with the cleaning crew.

Since getting her number, we'd spoken every night, and like high-school sweethearts, we talked until the early hours of the morning. Which we only regretted when we had to wake up for work the following day.

Latrice and I clicked better than I even thought we would, and Friday wasn't coming fast enough for me.

Latrice

11

When my doorbell rang, I had to force my hands to stop shaking. I was that nervous. Not so much about being on a date, which I hadn't been on in a while, but more the fact that I was going out with Vic—a white man. If my mother knew what I was doing, she'd scream murder. I'm sure Danita was watching me from above, just shaking her head and frowning with disapproval. I know I would have been the same way if the shoe were on the other foot.

Being attracted to Vic was something I never would have imagined happening. But as the saying goes—never say never. And what I said to Vic was true—he wasn't like the others; his upbringing had a lot to do with that. He grew up just like I did—one parent, poor, and determined. That's what set him apart from most of the white men I knew. It didn't hurt that his adoptive mother was a black woman and that he had an appreciation for black culture.

I put my hand on the doorknob and took a deep breath. *All right, girl, you said yes. You can do this; his skin color don't mean a thing.* I exhaled and opened the door.

With a Brad Pitt-like smile, Vic held out a bouquet of red roses and said, "Hey, Latrice."

I took the roses and inhaled their sweet fragrance. "Hey, yourself."

I watched Vic's eyes as he admired my outfit. I knew I was looking good. I had on a black skirt short enough to show off my legs, which I was extremely proud of, a red V-neck top, to accentuate the right amount of my ample cleavage, a string of pearls that Danita bought me once, and a pair of black pumps on my feet. I hid my smile as he smiled.

"You look good, Latrice."

"Good, huh?" I stepped to the side for him to come in. When he walked past me, I took a moment to check out what he had on—black pants with a baby-blue button-down shirt, covered by a black blazer. On his feet he wore a pair of black leather shoes. His outfit was simple and manly, and he looked damn sexy in it.

"You look good too."

"Thanks."

"Whew! Latrice, you have a nice set-up. Is that a Kebo Kante?" He walked over to where my cherry entertainment center sat with my thirty-six inch TV set and looked at the framed photograph on the wall—*Legs*. It was nothing more than a photo of a woman's shapely legs extended into the air and crossed at the ankles.

"I'm impressed. Not many people know about him."

"You mean not many *white* people?"

"No, I mean not *many* people. But, if you want to go there, then—yes, not many *white* people either."

"I have a couple of his prints. Photography was always a passion of my mother's. She used to have a Polaroid that she took everywhere she went. I mean, she would snap photos of anything—fire hydrants, kids playing, birds on a fence. I get my love of photography from her.

"I first ran into Kebo Kante's work when I was in California for a business meeting with my other company. I went to the Oakland Museum and was mesmerized when I saw his work."

"His work is very expressive; he says a lot with the lens."

"Yes, he does. I'm a big fan of his photomontage on wood. I have his book on it."

"I have that one on my coffee table. I have two more of his photographs, one in my bedroom, and the other in the bathroom."

"Why did you pick this one?"

"I used to be very heavy until a couple of years ago."

Vic's eyes widened.

"It's true." I suppressed a proud smile. "I was a very healthy girl."

"And what happened—not that I'm complaining?"

"My best friend, who was like my sister, passed away. I was so depressed, I just couldn't eat, couldn't sleep. Could barely function. One day, I got a really good look at myself in the mirror and saw for the first time how much I'd taken off. That day I decided to join the gym. So that particular photo is symbolic to me in the sense that never in a million years would I have thought that I would look the way I do today."

"Well, if my opinion matters . . . your legs are the ones that should be framed."

I smiled and batted my eyelashes. "Flattery will get you everywhere."

Vic gave another Brad Pitt smile and then moved to my CD collection. "You like a lot of music, I see."

"Music is what helps me wind down after a long day."

"Speaking of long," he said, turning toward me, "you ready for a long night?"

An hour later, we were sitting in the Rusty Scupper having dinner. Swallowing a sip of my lemonade, I said, "This place is nice. I've never been here. My girl, Danita, the one who passed away, came here. She told me all about how fancy it was." I looked through the glass to the ocean below us. I was definitely feeling the romantic mood created by the candlelight and piano music.

We talked for a while, mostly about work and all of the changes going on with the company, until our food came.

After we finished eating, we ordered cheesecake slices.

"I'm going to have to work double-time to get these calories off," I said.

"You won't have to work that hard; you hardly ate."

"I should have ordered the catfish instead of the steak, but I was just craving some red meat."

"It's not always a bad thing to give in to cravings every now and then."

"Mmm hmm," I said, getting the message.

We looked at each other for a hot second. Finally, Vic said, "Latrice, why don't you have a man?"

"What do you mean by that?"

"I mean, why isn't someone as attractive as yourself attached? What are the men doing wrong?"

I was glad my skin is the color of dark chocolate, or else he would have seen me blush. "I was involved with someone up until about a year ago."

"If you don't mind me asking—what happened?"

I shrugged my shoulders. "It just wasn't the right time, and we weren't the right people."

"I know exactly what you mean."

"But things always have a way of working out. I mean, let's face it—had he and I not broken up, you and I wouldn't be here tonight."

Vic smiled. "We better toast to our good fortune then."

We smiled and held each other's gaze for a few seconds; there was some definite chemistry going on.

"Just out of curiosity—have you heard from him since?"

I shook my head. "No. He's with someone else now."

"Good for him."

I couldn't help smiling. "It's nice to see you care about his feelings."

"Hey, he's a fellow male."

"Part of the male brotherhood, huh?"

"Exactly."

"So, anyway, since you asked me the personal 4-1-1—what's up with you and your wife—why the divorce?"

Vic cleared his throat. "It wasn't working out."

"*What* wasn't working out? You got married; it's not always going to work out."

"I wasn't happy."

"Oh, that's different then. Why weren't you happy?"

"Honestly, I initially married her because she was pregnant. I wanted to do right by the baby. I didn't want it growing up being split between two homes."

"And what—you changed your mind?"

"No. She miscarried."

"I'm sorry to hear that."

"Yeah. It was hard when it happened."

I sighed. "I got pregnant by my ex after my girl died. But with the stress, I lost it. That wasn't an easy thing to deal with. I know your wife must've taken it hard."

"Yeah, she did, but I made sure to be there, to help her through it."

"And you're still not happy?"

"Nope."

"And what will it take to make you happy?"

"An exceptional woman."

"I see. Have anyone in mind?"

"Just might."

"I see. So she could be exceptional, huh?"

"I'm sure she could be."

"'Could'?"

"I'm sure she would be."

"Mmm hmm—and why did you ask me out again?"

Vic laughed, and I followed suit. I was enjoying our flirtation. We went back and forth, dancing around what we both knew we wanted.

After paying for the check and leaving a generous tip, we left and went back to my place, where words were no longer needed. On the way there, I wondered if I could actually go through with being intimate with him. *I wonder if he would be able to get me going like so many brothers had.* I was nervous, but curious.

My apprehension quickly disappeared when he placed his lips on mine. From that moment, it was on. I caressed the tongue he offered and gave mine readily.

Before we could reach the bedroom, our clothes were off and scattered in a trail on the floor. When we finally reached the bed, we were already sweating and breathing heavily. I don't know about him, but it had been a while for me.

As he slid inside of me, all concerns about a white man's size and length flew out the window. While Vic worked some magic I had rarely experienced with even the finest of brothers, I let myself go and enjoyed the ride . . . until we both reached our destination.

Colin

12

There were a few things of mine no one could ever mess with—my family, my friends, my job, my possessions, and definitely not my groove. Messing with my groove was like a cardinal sin, punishable only by death. So when I was getting my groove on with Tanecia, whose name I had scribbled back into my book of conquests, and my doorbell rang, I was ready to go to jail. I tried to ignore the bell at first, but then the knocking started. When my phone went off and I saw who was calling, I was through. I turned my ringer off and ignored the knocking, which went on for another couple of minutes.

After it stopped, I threw my all into Tanecia until I released.

When she finally went home, after showering in my bathroom, I changed the sheets then picked up the phone and hit speed dial one. I yelled when he answered. "Vic, are you crazy? Don't you understand that when someone doesn't answer the door or the phone, they must be busy? What the hell were you thinkin', dog?"

"My bad. I figured you were sleeping," Vic said.

"'Sleeping'? Hell no, I wasn't sleeping! Dog, I had Tanecia in here. She was riding me like a champ. Man, you nearly screwed that up for me—again."

"Tanecia was there? The one who called you a dog? Damn, how'd you swing that?"

"Dog, you forget—I am Colin Ray—ain't a woman that can resist me. And believe me, I settled that dog shit quick. I laid some lines on her and it was over. She's back in the book. Now, again, what did you want? I need to catch some z's."

"Maaan! Colin, man!"

"What?"

"Man, I was with Latrice tonight."

"I know, fool. You told me and Roy you were going out with her."

"No, man. I mean I was *with* her."

"Oh. For real? You hit it?"

"Twice." Vic laughed out loud.

"'Twice'? Damn! It was that good?"

"Better. You think you were being ridden like a champ? Man. . ."

I couldn't hold back my laughter. "Man, that's good that you got some ass, because you were one wound-up fool these past couple of weeks. I bet you let all that stress out, huh?"

"Hell yeah, man. I was like a volcano."

"Right, right." I yawned. "So is that what you wanted, dog? . . . 'cause I can't front—I'm a worn-out nigga right about now—I need my beauty rest."

"Yeah, that's all, man. We're hooking up again tomorrow night."

I yawned and rubbed my eyes. "That's good." I could barely keep my eyes open. It was time for me to dream. "Yo, before I fall asleep on you, I'ma be out. I'll holla at you tomorrow."

"A'ight, man. Tomorrow then."

"Peace." I hung up the phone and got under the covers. I was asleep before the sheep count reached ten.

Latrice

13

"Girl, I have to skip the gym tonight," I said through the phone receiver.

"Skip the gym?" Emily asked. "You never skip the gym. You okay? Is something wrong?"

"Girl, I am better than okay. Vic is taking me to an exhibit at the museum tonight."

"You're going out with him again? Damn, you guys have been at it for about four months now. Don't you two get tired of one another? I mean, you see him at work too."

I sucked my teeth and applied my lipstick. I was excited for the date tonight. Kebo Kante was having a special showing of his work at the museum in DC. Vic found out about it through a friend of his. Getting tickets last minute the way he did, I figured he had to have gotten them illegally, but I didn't ask. All that mattered was that he got them, and he wanted to take me.

Being with Vic made my day. I loved the spirited

conversations we had. More importantly, I loved the fact that he could hold his own against my attitude and stubbornness. It was nice to be around a man who wasn't intimidated by me, and four months wasn't nearly long enough.

"Girl, I don't get tired of him at all. Besides, since we started talking we don't see each other at work like that anymore. We figured it'd be better that way, so no one is all in our business."

"Good move. I know all about nosy people and the rumors they like to spread. I deal with that twenty-four/seven at the office."

"Oh, I know you do."

"So you think he could be the one?"

"I don't know about the one—yet. But, Em, Vic is caring, intelligent, sensitive, and fun to be with."

"And his being white doesn't bother you?"

"Girl, he has rhythm." I laughed out loud and then did one last double-take in the mirror. I was looking good. I had on a long, black dress that snuggled against my curves, and earlier that day I'd had my braids re-done. "Seriously, though, the color issue is dead; he's just a good man."

"Well, I still haven't met him."

"Girl, I know. You will, though. Soon."

"I'm not pressed. Just want to check him out. Anyway, I'm glad you like him, and I'm glad that race isn't an issue." Emily sighed.

I turned off the bathroom light and walked into the living room. I felt bad. Emily had broken up with her man just a week before I first went out with Vic. I knew she was lonely, and hearing about my good fortune wasn't exactly her idea of fun. "Hey, girl, why don't we skip the gym tomorrow and go on a shopping spree during the day?" I suggested.

"Sure, we can do that. What about tomorrow night . . . you doing anything?"

I hesitated before I answered. "Yeah . . . I'm going out with Vic tomorrow night."

Emily sighed. "Oh, okay."

There was silence for a few seconds, and then I said, "Hey, instead of waiting, why don't you join us tomorrow night?"

"What—and be the third wheel?—I don't think so."

"No, girl. Vic has a friend, Colin, who I heard would be interested in meeting you."

Emily's voice picked up. "He cute?"

"You know I wouldn't set you up with no dog. Besides, Vic calls him a pretty boy."

"'Pretty boy'? You know I like my men a little rough around the edges."

"Girl, you going or not?—let me know; Vic is gonna be here soon."

Emily huffed, but I could tell she was excited. "Yeah, I'll go . . . as long as Vic's friend is down."

"Oh he is, girl."

As I hung up the phone, I shook my head. From what I'd heard about Colin, he seemed like a cool guy. Vic said they were boys since junior high school. I hoped Vic could convince him to go out on a blind date.

When Vic rang my bell, I decided not to beat around the bush. "I told my girl Emily that she could come out with us tomorrow night. I hope you don't mind."

Vic looked at me and smiled. "It's cool. Gives me a chance to meet her. I feel like I know her, as much as you talk about her."

"Emily is cool. You and her are a lot alike—a lot."

"Cool. I hope she doesn't mind being the 'third wheel.'" Vic slipped my coat around my shoulders.

Without looking at him, I said, "Oh, she's not going to be the third wheel."

"Oh, she's not? She has a date?"

"Yeah."

"That's cool. Leaves me free to put all my attention on you. Is her date a nice guy? I know you said she just recently broke up with her man."

I closed and locked my front door. "He sounds nice . . . at least from the way you describe him."

Vic stopped walking when I said that.

I continued on to the car.

From behind me, I heard him say, "The way I describe him?—what do you mean by that?" He hurried up to me and touched my shoulder. "Latrice, what did you mean, from the way I describe him?"

My shoulders slumped. "I told her that your friend Colin wanted to take her out."

Vic stared at me and raised an eyebrow. "You what?"

"Vic, she asked me what I was doing, and when I said we were going out, she sounded so down. I couldn't leave her hanging, so I told her your friend wanted to take her out. I'm sorry, boo; it just sort of slipped out."

"'Sort of slipped out'? I'd say it slipped out. Latrice, as much as I care about you, there is no way I'm going to set your girl up with Colin."

"Why?" I rested my hands on my hips. "What— you think I'll set your boy up with some fugly-ass chick?"

"No, Latrice, I know you wouldn't. It's just that . . . well . . . you wouldn't understand."

"Well, then help me understand." I got in his Eclipse. I was getting angry. Emily was my girl, and I wanted to help her out. I would have expected Vic to go along with that without a problem. When he got in, I said, "What—you think Emily isn't good enough for your friend?"

"Latrice, I'm not worried about her being good enough—that's the least of my worries."

"So what is it, then?"

"Latrice, Colin is my boy, but he is a player's player. He is interested in only one thing from a woman. It wouldn't be right of me to set her up with Colin. Besides, he would never go for a blind date. Colin is way too stuck on himself to go there like that."

"Look, Emily is a big girl; she can handle herself. I'm sure she's dealt with men like Colin before. All I want is for her to get out of the house and enjoy herself. He doesn't have to take her out again."

"I'm telling you—Colin would never go for it."

"You saying that he wouldn't be willing to do one small favor for his boy?"

"No, I'm not saying that."

"Well, good—it's settled then. We'll go out for a bite to eat and then go dancing. Your boy can dance, can't he?"

Vic grumbled and then started the ignition.

I dropped the last bomb on him. "Oh, by the way, Emily is white, but she's like you—she has soul. Anyway, I'm sure her skin color won't be a problem for Colin."

Vic looked at me and shook his head.

With a smile, I turned on his radio. I know he wanted to protest even more, but I wasn't trying to hear it. I had to get Emily out the house. As Janet Jackson sang about how "it didn't really matter," I nodded my head. It didn't really matter to me one way or the other how his friend felt. All I knew was, he better show up for the date.

Vic drove the car and didn't say a word until we got to the museum.

The rest of the date went as smooth as silk. That night, we capped it off with another bout of headboard-banging sex.

In the morning, as he was leaving, I reminded him to talk to his friend.

Vic

14

We were in the mall checking out some females and buying a few things in the process.

"Somebody slap Vic and wake him up! Man, you have got to be trippin'!" Colin exclaimed.

I lowered my head and mumbled, "No, man. I'm not tripping."

"Roy, please tell this boy he better go out and find some lonely fool that has no plans and no life, because the one thing I don't do are blind dates."

Roy looked at me and shrugged his shoulders. "You knew he'd say that."

I gave him a cross look, thanking him for his input and then looked back to Colin.

"Colin man, just do this one favor for me. I don't always come to you like this. It's only for a couple of hours."

"Vic, save your begging for somebody else. There is no way in hell I am going out on some blind date."

"Colin, come on. Don't act like I've never done

shit before for you. Just do this for me, man. Believe me, it wasn't my idea. Latrice already told her friend you wanted to take her out."

Colin stared at me.

I cracked my knuckles. I knew what his reaction was going to be. I knew it the moment Latrice let me know that Colin saying no wasn't an option. I had as much chance getting him to agree to go as Mike Tyson had of winning a "humanitarian of the year" award. My only hope was that somehow he would have my back. I looked at Roy and without words, asked for some help.

Roy looked at me and put his palms in the air.

I gave him another thanks-for-nothing look.

"Vic, you better tell your girl to tell her friend she was mistaken. Because you are shit out of luck asking me to go." Colin swallowed the rest of his hot dog and picked up his bags; he was ready to go.

I looked again to Roy, who was swallowing the last of his chilidog.

Finally, he cleared his throat and said, "Colin, can't you do him this one favor? He would do it for you, you know that." I nodded my head emphatically. "All he's asking for is one night, man. Help him out."

Colin looked over at Roy. "Nigga, did you drink from the same well that fool was drinkin' from? You really expect me to go on some blind date, and set myself up to be sittin' next to some ugly chick?"

"Yo, Latrice said that her friend is cute."

"Of course, she did! What—you think she's gonna admit that her friend could probably run neck and neck with a pit bull? Man, she's setting her friend up on a blind date—what do you think that means?"

"She wouldn't say her friend was cute if she wasn't. Come on, Colin. Remember when I had your back when that girl you met at DC Live tried to go off on you? Who was there to back up your lies? Who was there when you set up two dates on the same night and forgot about them? Man, just do this one thing for me."

"Why you gonna bring up old shit? Man, at least I didn't ask you to go out with some chick you ain't never seen before. I wouldn't do that to you, dog. Friends don't do that to each other."

Roy cleared his throat again. "Colin, I hear where you're coming from, but I have to say, man, friends would help their friends when they're in a bind."

"Man, go and buy another chilidog." Colin walked away.

I looked at Roy and frowned.

Then my eyes widened—he knew what I was thinking. Very quickly, he said, "Hey, I might be having problems, but I'm still married—don't even think about it."

Damn! How was I going to tell Latrice that Colin wouldn't go? I sighed.

Roy came up to me and patted me on the shoulder. "Who knows, maybe having a third wheel won't be so bad."

I groaned.

A few steps ahead of us, Colin stopped walking. He didn't turn around as he said, "I'll be by your place at seven, but Vic, I swear, you are gonna owe me big time for this."

I went up to my boy and extended my hands. "Thanks, man. I knew you wouldn't leave me hanging."

Colin took my hand and gave me a pound. "No—you *hoped* and *prayed* I wouldn't leave you hanging."

"Yeah, that too."

We all laughed, then Roy said, "See, Vic, you were wrong—he just might have a decent bone in his body."

"Yeah, okay, big boy. You may want to lay off the chilidogs from now on, or else Stacey is going to kick your ass out," Colin joked.

"'Bruh, please . . . with each day that goes by, she falls more and more in love with my 'love belly.'" Roy laughed, and so did I.

But I had to admit, "Roy, you are putting on some weight there."

"Fellas, I have a wife, two little girls, and a mortgage. I think I'm entitled. Besides, your asses aren't the ones I'm lying next to at night, so as long as my wife approves, I have nothing to worry about."

The three of us laughed and chilled in the mall for another half-hour. Then we left to prepare for the evening ahead.

Roy went to rent a couple of movies for his family, Colin went to make a few backup calls for after the blind date, and I went home to chill and get ready.

I still hadn't told Colin about Emily's skin color. That wasn't going to be pretty.

Colin

15

The only reason I agreed to go out with Vic was because he was my boy. Besides, what Roy said was true—Vic would have done it for me. But I still wasn't happy about it, because I had planned on calling Tanecia again, which would have been a real first for me, since I'd just had her in my bed earlier in the week. She wasn't the smartest cookie on the planet, but she damn sure knew how to work the middle. Besides, I was horny as hell. Vic asking me to go on the blind date quickly killed that though. I knew I was going to say yes the minute he asked me. I couldn't leave him hanging. He really seemed to be into this Latrice chick, who none of us had seen yet, and I was curious to know just how fine she was. Vic always did have good taste in women. Julie was fine, so I didn't really have any doubts that Latrice would be too.

Shit, although I never considered dating a white female, knowing what I know now about Julie, if I could go back in time, I may have been tempted to make a play at her . . . maybe. Now, if she were a sister, no doubt, I would have scooped her up without hesitation. I'm not saying I would have married her, but I would have definitely put triple stars beside her name in my book. By no means was I racist; I just loved black women, and it was going to take a lot for me to go out with a white female, no matter how bad she was.

Speaking of taking a lot—there was no way I was going to let Vic forget about my sacrifice to go on the blind date. That's something I had never done, never planned on doing, and couldn't believe I was about to do now. I'd heard too many horror stories of guys who'd heard the sweet voice over the phone and seen a beast in public. I would never let Vic live it down if his girl's friend was Medusa reincarnated. The sad thing was, all Vic could tell me was that he heard she was cute. *Cute?* Puppies, kittens, little kids—these are cute things. A cute woman, in my book, was nothing more than an ugly woman with a nice personality. And while a nice personality was cool, it did nothing for me in the sack.

That's why I had my backup plan worked out. Instead of calling Tanecia, I called another hottie and told her I wanted to hook up later that night. I met her at the grocery store a while back. She was a fine, intelligent caramel sister with a good job, no man, no kids, ass for weeks, and, to top it off, she was a freeeeak. She had me curling *my* toes from the sexual trip we took. The only female who came close was Tanecia. If I wasn't so unwilling to commit, maybe I'd take the time to try and find one woman to satisfy me sexually and mentally.

But commitment and I went together like oil and water—we just weren't compatible.

I'd never been able to commit when it came to women; that and my looks were the only traits I got from my father. He was a non-committing fool, if there ever was one—that's why he and my mother never made it to the altar. Other than those similarities, we were complete opposites. Even though he was getting better in his old age, my father still had a teenager's mentality. He wouldn't recognize responsibility if it smacked him hard on the back of his bald dome. I couldn't remember the last time he held a steady job or had any kind of meaningful relationship with anybody other than the 'ho's he dealt with. And I say 'ho's, because some of the chicks he'd had, I'd had.

My father was in his fifties, but looked like he was in his thirties. He didn't know about the ladies we'd shared, and they'd never said a word to him. I think they liked having been with father and son. Like I said—'ho's.

My dad and I didn't speak too often. Actually, we only spoke when he called to borrow some money. He lived in a beat-up two-bedroom apartment in DC with some crackhead-looking chick named Mo. I lent him the money only because he was my pops. Other than that, I didn't deal with him.

I couldn't say the same about my younger brother and business partner, Mike. He cut our father off from the moment he was old enough to realize what type of man he didn't want to be. He and my father hadn't spoken in years, and I doubted whether Mike would've even visited his grave.

So, just like I played the Good Samaritan to my old man, I was doing the same for Vic.

"I swear, man, if she's ugly you won't live this down." I climbed into my Lincoln Navigator. I had just gotten the new ride a couple of weeks back, so I chose to drive. Besides, if by some slim chance Latrice's friend was in fact cute, I would at least be representing myself properly.

"She'll be all right, man; Latrice wouldn't do me like that," Vic assured me.

"Yeah—exactly—but what would she do to *me*?"

"It'll be cool, man. Her friend goes with her to the gym."

"To maintain a fine figure, or to find a figure?"

"Man, just chill. The night's gonna be okay."

"Yeah, we'll see. So what do you have planned anyway, Romeo?—and I assume you're payin', right, 'cause I didn't bring my wallet?"

Vic gave me a you've-got-to-be-kidding look.

"You for real?"

"What do you mean, am I for real?" I struggled to keep from smiling. "I'm doing you a favor. You thought I was going to spend my money on someone I don't know? The real question is—are *you* for real?"

Vic mumbled something under his breath.

"What was that?"

Quietly, Vic said, "I got you; I just need to stop at the ATM."

I could tell by the reddening of his cheeks that he was frustrated. I couldn't hold it back any longer. I busted out laughing. "Just kiddin', dog. Ha! I had your ass worried . . . although I should make your ass pay."

Vic smiled. "Nah."

"Yeah, okay. So, anyway, what's the plan?"

"We're gonna meet them at Angelo and Maxie's Steakhouse for dinner and then head to Zanzibar."

"Damn, man! Angelo and Maxie's? That place is not cheap. I'm not trying to spend a grip for some female I don't know."

"The food there is good, man."

"You are definitely going to owe me for this."

"Yeah, yeah. And you won't forget either."

"Damn right, I won't forget."

We laughed and then got quiet. I had the volume turned up on the radio. We were both grooving to the Ja Rule and Jennifer Lopez collaboration.

When the song finished, I lowered the radio. "You know something," I said, cruising down 295, "I don't even know this chick's name."

"Oh, my bad. I completely forgot—it's Emily."

"'Emily'?—funny name for a sister. Whatever . . . just as long as she's not ugly."

Vic was quiet for the rest of the ride, until we got to the restaurant. Since the ladies hadn't arrived yet, we decided to chill outside for a few. The night air was crisp, but bearable. I did zip my jacket up though, while Vic had his draped over his arm.

"This is about the only time I could really accuse you of being white," I said.

Vic looked at me. "What do you mean?"

"Man, I swear, it could be fifty below, and white people would still be out in shorts and T-shirts."

Vic laughed. "It's not cold, man."

"No, but it's chilly enough for a jacket. Why did you bring yours if you weren't gonna wear it?"

"Just in case I do get cold."

"That's my point—you won't get cold. Y'all never get cold. I mean, is it the lack of pigmentation that keeps y'all warm?"

Vic and I laughed, and then laughed even harder as a white couple walked by hand in hand. They both had on shorts and sandals, and were shivering. I looked at Vic, who shrugged his shoulders.

We stood outside for another twenty minutes and the ladies still hadn't showed. I was ready to leave. "Man, are you sure they're coming?"

"They're women; they'll be here."

I exhaled. I could never stand a woman that took forever to get ready. I turned around and looked down F Street and saw two women strolling in our direction. One was a fine sister with a body that made me go, "Mmm mmm." The other was a white female with an equally fine body and cornrows. "I'll tell you what," I said, rubbing my palms together, "if your chick and her friend don't get here soon, I may have to scoop up that fine sister coming this way."

Vic turned around. "That's them."

I looked down F Street again. "Who's them?"

"Latrice and Emily."

I stared at the two women. Keeping my eye on them, I said, "Vic, one of those females is white." When he didn't say anything, I turned and faced him. "Vic, one of those females is white," I said again.

Vic cleared his throat and looked down.

"Aww, man! I can't believe this shit! How are you gonna do me like this, man? I'm supposed to be your boy. Man, you know I don't date white females."

In a low voice, he said, "Man, I know. I'm sorry I didn't tell you. But I knew you wouldn't have come if you knew."

"Damn right, I wouldn't have come. Damn!"

"It's only one night, man."

"Vic, I don't date white females—not even attractive ones."

"Man, it's just dinner."

"Yeah. And then you're talkin' about Zanzibar afterwards. Bruh, have you lost your mind? As many females—no, sisters as I know, what you think is going to happen when I stroll in the club with a white girl on my arm? Man! Are you tryin' to take me out of the game?"

"Colin, man, I'm sorry."

I started, "Oh, you're sorry, all right—"

"Baby!" Latrice walked up to Vic and kissed him. "Sorry we're so late, but you know we had to make sure we looked good."

Keeping his eyes on me, Vic said, "It's cool. We haven't been here too long." Then he looked at her and said, "It was worth the wait anyway. You are looking damn good."

Latrice smiled and said, "Don't I know it." Then she turned toward me and extended her hand. "We've never met, but as much as Vic talks about his boys, I feel like I know you already—Latrice Meadows."

I shook her hand and forced a smile. "Colin

Ray. Nice to finally meet the woman who's been drivin' my boy insane." I looked at Vic with a deadpan glare.

Latrice smiled and said, "Nice to meet you too." Then she took her friend's arm and pulled her forward.

"Excuse me for being rude. Everyone, this is Emily. Emily, this fine man on the left is Vic, who you already know all about, and this brother, as you heard, is Colin."

Emily smiled at Vic. "To repeat the sentiments of your friend, it's nice to finally meet the one who's been driving my girl insane."

Everyone laughed, except for me.

Then Emily turned to me and extended her hand. "Nice to meet you, Colin."

It seemed as though time stood still while I contemplated my move. The right side of my brain was telling me to jet, hook up with Denise, and do something truly artistic. Unfortunately, the analytical side was reasoning with me. I couldn't leave my friend hanging like that—although he had done that to me by not telling me about Emily.

I took her hand in mine and said, "Likewise, Emily." When I let go, I gave Vic another cross look and then said, "Why don't we go inside." *Because I don't want anyone to recognize me*, I wanted to add. But I kept that thought to myself, and thought about my backup plan later on. But believe it or not, it never happened.

Latrice

16

"**Y**ou what?" I sat up in the bed as Vic was snuggling next to me. I quickly remembered to keep my voice down, but it was hard to do, especially after what Emily just told me. "What did you just say, girl?"

"I said I just slept with Colin. He just left my place," Emily said.

I got out of the bed and went into the living room, where I wouldn't have to worry about being quiet. Sitting on my sofa, I said, "Girl, why did you do that? I told you what a dog he was."

"Latrice, I appreciate you looking out for me, but seriously, I'm a big girl."

"Oh, you're big, huh? Big enough to sleep with a dog like Colin, right?"

"That's right, Latrice—I am that big."

I sucked my teeth. I was mad. Colin was a nice guy, but I could tell he was the type of brother who liked to hit and run. He was fine—there was no doubt about that—and successful, but like Vic said, he was a player. That made him ugly in my book. I was disappointed in Emily.

"Damn, Em, I know you were horny, but why'd you go out like that? You only met him once. And that was last week. Speaking of which . . . how the hell did you hook up with him anyway? I don't remember you two exchanging numbers, and I know he didn't ask Vic for it, because Vic didn't ask me."

"We exchanged numbers the night we all went out. We've been speaking since then."

"When? I don't remember seeing that. And what do you mean 'speaking'?"

"We traded numbers while you and Vic were getting your freak on at Zanzibar. And I mean 'speaking' as in on the phone—every day since Saturday."

I stood up and went to the window. I looked out to the quiet neighborhood before me. I'm sure if I opened my window, my voice, along with the crickets, would be the only sound that could be heard. I couldn't believe they had been talking and she hadn't said anything. "Why are you now telling me this?"

"Didn't want to say anything until I knew it was real."

"'Real'? Girl, how many different females' numbers you think he has?"

"Latrice, I don't care about them. Why are you giving me such a hard time over this? I thought you would be happy that I'm happy. You're the one who's always saying I need to go out and find a man to release some stress. I finally do that, and now you're tripping."

I turned away from the window. "Em, I said find

a man, not a dog. Girl, I just think you're better than the tricks Colin has probably hooked up with. I don't want you to be another notch on his bed-post."

"Latrice, I love you, but I am really capable of taking care of myself. Besides, how do you know I'm not more than another notch? How do you know he doesn't like me like that? We talk through-out the day, and we talk until the late hours of the night. How do you know something couldn't be happening with us?"

"Please, Em," I said, sitting back on the couch, "don't even go there. Men like Colin are not capa-ble of being in any kind of a relationship past a sexual one. Now, if you want to be in that kind of a relationship, you go right ahead, but don't even try to think it could lead to anything more than that."

"Latrice, you may not want to believe this, but I think Colin really likes me. We've shared some deep things this week."

"Please . . . like he doesn't have some of those things rehearsed for other women."

"Stop being so negative!"

It actually made me stop moving and stare at my phone.

Emily continued before I could go off on her for defending a dog. "Do you know that he wasn't happy when he first saw me?"

"Why?"

"Because I'm white."

"'White'? Vic is white."

"He's never dated a white woman before."

"How do you know? I find that hard to believe."

"Because he told me so."

"Don't be so naïve, Emily, for real; you know how brothers do nowadays."

"I'm not naive. What he said was true."

"So if he doesn't like going out with white women, why'd he come?"

"Because your man never told him I was white. He said if Vic had told him, he never would have agreed to come. Which, by the way, means you were lying to me when you said he wanted to go out with me."

I huffed into the receiver. "Sorry, girl. I just wanted you out of the house."

"I forgive you. I wouldn't have met Colin if it weren't for your lie anyway."

"You can't like him like that, Em. You don't want to like a man like him."

"Latrice . . . "

"Okay, okay. Not another negative comment." *Out loud*, I thought. I still wasn't happy about it and was sure to let Vic know about it.

"Do you know he had another date lined up for later that evening?"

"I told you, girl, men like that—"

"He'd never done a blind date before, Latrice. He had another date lined up in case I was ugly; I would have done the same thing—either that or pretended to be sick."

"Oh, I've done that before."

"See, so why are you getting on him?"

She had me there.

"He's been really honest with me, Latrice—that's what I like about him—he doesn't beat around the bush, and he's not fake. He knows I know about his player's card. And he doesn't try to hide that."

"So why you wanna waste your time?"

"Latrice . . ."

"I mean, are you sure you want to get involved with him?"

"Girl, I'm not sure of what exactly I want right now, but I do know this—I'm comfortable talking to Colin. We have great conversations. And I have to be honest—he is no joke in bed. He earned his degree."

"Girl," I said smiling, "you know you gonna have to give me those details."

"I will. Later. I'm tired right now. And if I plan on going to work tomorrow, I better get some sleep. I just wanted to call and tell you what happened before Colin told Vic."

"Give me a taste, girl. You know how I am."

Emily laughed like I hadn't heard her laugh in a while. "All right, but this is all I'm giving you for now."

"Until later."

"Yeah, until later. Anyway, I am not exaggerating when I say that the brother is skilled with the tongue. See you tomorrow, Latrice."

Before I could beg for more, Emily hung up the phone. As I stood up, Vic called my name. I walked into the bedroom and stared at my sexy man, who was propped up on his elbows.

"You were on the phone?" He looked at the time.

"Yeah. Emily called me. You were knocked out and didn't hear it ring." I put the phone back in the base, climbed into bed, and straddled him. I could feel him start to grow almost instantly. I liked that I had that effect on him.

"Is there a problem?" he asked, taking one of my breasts in his hand.

I moaned. I loved the way he caressed me. "There better not be," I said softly.

"What do you mean?" he said, taking me into his mouth.

"I mean Colin better not be trying to dog my girl. They've been talking. And she just had sex with him."

Vic stopped his sucking and squeezing and looked at me. "What did you say?"

"I said your boy who doesn't like white girls has been talking to Emily and just sexed her around the town."

Vic opened his mouth to speak, but I put my index finger on his lips. "We'll talk about that later," I whispered. His throbbing had me wet. I moved from on top of him, and removed my shirt and underwear. Lying back on the bed, I opened my legs and exposed all of my flesh to him.

Following the calling of my finger, he removed his pants and eased his way in between my thighs. Never removing his mouth from my own, he attempted to guide himself into my sweetness.

I stopped him and shook my head. I pointed to my cavern as he looked at me. "Those lips want a kiss too."

He nodded and then made his way down.

When we were both satisfied, we lay in each other's arms. I'm sure Colin was good, but Vic was a master in his own right.

Colin

17

As soon as Vic opened his door, I knew he knew. *Damn.* And then, when I walked in and saw Roy staring at me, I knew he knew too. *Double damn.* I walked in, took my leather coat off, and threw it on the couch beside me as I sat down. Nobody said a word. The TV was on and set to FOX for the game. I grabbed a beer, opened it, and took a long sip.

Roy and Vic continued to stare at me—the move was mine to make.

I stared at the TV. John Madden and Pat Summerall were giving the pre-game hype for the Redskins-Cowboys second match-up of the year. I tried to focus on the screen and ignore the attention I was getting, but there was no way to do that.

"Okay," I said as a commercial came on, "yeah, I hooked up with Emily last night."

Vic turned off the TV. "Man, how the hell did that happen, Mr. I-don't-date-white-females?"

"Yeah, how the hell did it happen . . . because

from what Vic was telling me, you were ready to go to blows when you saw her?" Roy added.

I looked at my boys and shook my head. "Man, will you turn the TV back on."

"Forget the game," Vic said. "The Cowboys are going to kick ass again anyway; the game is the least important thing right now."

"When did you find out?" I asked.

"She called Latrice at three this morning."

I sighed. *Damn, she told her girl that quick.*

Hooking up with Emily was the last thing I would have ever expected happening . . . especially after I saw her. I wanted to snap on Vic for real. It's not that I had anything against white women; it's just that I was always brought up to respect and cherish black women. From my mother to my grandmother, black women were always the "queens," and I was supposed to be the proud and strong king. I may hold top seat in "Playerville," but I always ran my game on the sisters. I never strayed—until that night. I don't know how it happened, but somehow I ended up having one of the best times I'd had in a long time. Maybe the fact that Emily, for a white female, was "down" had something to do with my digging her.

All I know is as the night went on, her race became unimportant to me. I was feeling her on a level I had never felt. She was cool, and I couldn't front—she had a fine body and ass that most white women just didn't have. I was also feeling the cornrows in her hair. But more than her body or her light blue eyes, which seemed to sparkle, or the rows, I was really feeling her mindset. She was intelligent and had some positive and insightful thoughts on a number of topics, ranging from race and religion, to the worth of women in society, and amazingly enough, to the plight of the black dating experience in the 2000's—especially for women.

We were chilling by the bar at Zanzibar, while Latrice and Vic were out on the dance floor. Although I enjoyed the conversation at the restaurant, I was reluctant to go out on the dance floor with her. And even though I watched her shaking her hips smoothly to a Missy Elliott groove, I still wasn't willing to see if she could hold her own on the floor. I also didn't want anyone who knew me to see me with her like that—that was like death for a brother, because when black women saw a brother with a white female, he could forget about being respected. So I was content to just chill and talk to her, while I had a beer and Emily had a Long Island Iced Tea.

We were joking about a skinny brother dancing with a woman who could probably have eaten him and had seconds, when out of the blue Emily said, "Colin, I know you don't want to dance with me because I'm white, so if you see a good-looking black woman, you can go ahead and make your player move."

I looked at her. "What makes you think that?"

"Oh please . . . you think I didn't see how uncomfortable you were earlier when you first saw me? I'm not blind, you know, nor am I stupid. But it's all good."

I was impressed that she had seen right through me. "Is it?"

"Yeah, it is. I understand how hard it is for black men to legitimately talk to women of another race."

"Oh, do you?" I turned and faced her. "And how do you understand that?"

"Oh, come on . . . it's common knowledge that black women can't stand when a black man talks to a woman outside of their race. They catch immediate attitudes when they see that. And when that happens, it's all over for the brother. No matter how sweet or sensitive or positive he may be, he is nothing but a sell-out in the eyes of the sisters—that's not fair to the man."

I sipped on my Heineken and stroked my goatee. "I see," I said, intrigued by her understanding. "But can you blame them for being upset about it? I mean, if you ask the sisters where all the good black men are, they'll tell you they're with white women. The majority of them feel that way. So can you really blame them when they give attitude?"

Emily shook her head. "Uh uh, I don't blame them at all; I sympathize with them actually."

I liked the way her cornrows dangled behind her neck. "'Sympathize'? How is that?"

"Look at me, Colin—it's obvious that I'm no average, run-of-the-mill white girl. I grew up in the projects in New York. Really, I'm no different from Latrice, which is why we get along so well."

"Okay, but you still haven't told me how you sympathize with black women."

"I understand their frustration because whenever Latrice and I go out, I'm always the one the brothers stare at first."

"And that frustrates you?"

"Yeah, it does. See, I know that I'm not ugly, but I also know that I'm not as attractive as Latrice. The only reason brothers give me 'play' is because of my skin color. That's frustrating to me because, one, I don't want to be admired for my skin color, and two, I don't like to see a beautiful woman like Latrice get picked second because of my skin color. So I sympathize with black women and their annoyance over brothers who pass them up."

I drank some more of my beer. I didn't say a word for a little while as I thought about what she'd said.

A few minutes later, Latrice and Vic came over for a break. "Girl, I need to use the bathroom," Latrice said, taking Emily's arm. "Come on. We'll be back."

When they left, Vic looked at me. Beads of sweat trickled down his forehead. This was our first moment alone all night.

I handed him a napkin. "So you gettin' your groove on, huh?"

He took it and wiped his face. "Yeah, man. We always get it on like that. Latrice can shake that ass for sure."

"I bet she can."

"So what's up, man? What do you think of her?"

"Oh, she's cool, dog, real cool. I'll be honest—I was shocked she was as fine as she was. It's not that I thought you would end up with an ugly chick. It's just that, despite her color, Julie was high on my scale of measurement for females. I didn't think you were going to come as close to surpassing her as you have. You and Latrice seem to fit pretty well too. She has the right amount of attitude to match your personality. I'm happy for you, dog; you have my approval."

Vic shook his head. "That's cool, man, but that's not who I was talking about; I meant Emily."

"Emily?"

"Yeah."

I sipped on my beer and shrugged my shoulders. After all of the hollering I did about not being into white women, I decided not to tell him how intrigued I was. "She's a'ight. Nothin' special. Typical, you know."

"So you're not gonna dance with her?"

"Hell no! Dog, are you crazy? You know I can't be out there like that."

"Okay, man. Just thought it would be better than standing to the side watching me and Latrice."

"Man, I'm not watchin' y'all. I been checkin' honeys out all night."

Just then, Latrice and Emily came back. Latrice smiled and took Vic's arm. "You ready?"

"Whenever you are."

Without saying goodbye, they disappeared back out on the floor.

"They're good together, aren't they?" Emily asked.

I was actually glad that Emily was back. "Yeah, they're cool."

We stood silent then, just watching people get down and listening to the jams that were being played. I wanted to dance but just couldn't bring myself to do it.

A couple of songs later, I did something that

shocked me all the way home. I turned to Emily and said, "So . . . are we going to exchange numbers?"

Emily looked at me and smiled. "And what would we be exchanging numbers for?"

"To continue our discussion."

"Oh, I see. In that case, do you have a pen?"

I reached in my pocket and removed my cell phone. "I'll put it in here."

Emily took her phone out. "I'll put yours in here."

I took her number down, and for the rest of the night we just chilled and talked.

My backup plan never came to fruition that night. Instead, I went home and did something I hadn't done in a long while—sleep alone on a Saturday night.

Emily and I spoke frequently after that. If she wasn't calling me, I was calling her. Our conversations were always long and spirited. We had planned on hooking up at her place. At first, I didn't want anyone to know because I wasn't quite sure I was in the right frame of mind. I didn't actually plan on sleeping with her, but I had gone to her place prepared with a new box of condoms. I went by her house because I didn't want anyone to see her by my place.

We rented a movie and ordered pizza and wings. We talked for a while, and then while the movie played, we explored each other. After our night together, I told her I didn't care if anyone knew.

* * *

"Yeah, a'ight, man, it happened."

"Well, I'll be damned!" Roy jumped up and laughed. "Colin went over to the other side."

"Shut up, man. I didn't go over to any side; I'm still me."

Vic elbowed Roy. "How many times have you guys spoken?"

I looked at them. "Why you wanna know?"

"What? You can't say?" Vic smiled.

"Yeah, Colin, what's up with that?"

I took a sip of beer. "Fools, we're missing the game."

"So answer the question," Vic insisted.

I exhaled, stood up, and hit the switch on the TV. "I talked to her all week," I said as I sat down.

As they dapped each other and laughed, I stared at the screen. The Redskins were actually winning, but I didn't really care. I was thinking about Emily, and the magic she worked with her hips.

Roy

18

"I saw Julie today," Stacey said as she brushed Jenea's hair. Sheila was watching TV, waiting her turn, and I was at the table going over a few bills.

"Oh yeah? How's she doing?" I asked, unhappily writing out a check for the gas and electric bill. Winter months were when I really hated paying bills.

"She's been seeing somebody—Jenea, will you keep still; I'm almost finished."

"Sorry, Mommy."

I made a funny face at her, making her giggle.

"Good for her," I said to Stacey. "Whoever he is, he's a lucky man; Julie's a good catch."

"Too bad your boy didn't know that."

I didn't comment, not wanting to get into another argument with her. We'd been doing a lot of arguing lately. And as Colin had predicted, the sex had stopped and I was spending the occasional night on the couch.

"Speaking of your boy," Stacey said, "is he still dating that Latrine girl?"

I looked at her disapprovingly from the corner of my eye. "It's *Latrice*, and yeah, he's still dating her."

"Humph . . . she must be special," Stacey said with attitude.

"She's pretty cool."

"So was Julie."

I put my pen down and looked at my wife. She was just finishing with Jenea's braids and had an angry scowl on her face. I shook my head and said, "We're having a get-together this Saturday night."

Stacey looked at me. "What do you mean, 'we're having a get-together'? "

"I mean, I invited Vic, Latrice, Colin, and his new friend Emily over to watch the Tyson fight."

"And when were you planning on telling me this?"

"I'm telling you now."

"How do you know I didn't have anything planned for Saturday, Roy? I mean, this is a marriage; you could have discussed this with me."

I rose from the table and went to the kitchen to get a glass of water. When I came back I said, "Stacey, I'm not about to get into another argument with you, okay?"

"Then treat me like your equal and discuss things with me before you make plans."

"Stacey, what is your problem? It's never been a big deal for the fellas to come over before. Why are you snapping? Please don't tell me it has anything to do with Vic coming here."

Stacy looked at the girls. "Girls, go to your room

please. Sheila, I'll do your hair in a couple of minutes."

Too used to the sounds of our arguing, Jenea and Sheila quickly disappeared.

When I heard the door slam shut, I massaged my temples. I could feel the headache coming on as Stacey got up and approached me. "First of all," she said, strangling the comb she was using, "I don't appreciate you coming off at me like that in front of the girls. Second of all, I wasn't snapping. All I said was I would appreciate it if you talked to me first before inviting your friends over here. And, yes, it has everything to do with Vic being here."

I watched her as she held the comb like she wanted to hit me with it. "Listen, Stacey," I said, forcing my voice to stay calm, "I'm tired of going through this with you. What went on between Vic and Julie was none of our business. It's ridiculous that you can't continue to be his friend just because he no longer has feelings for her. You act as though he fell out of love with you. I am through going back and forth with you. I can't even mention Vic's name without you catching an attitude. That has to stop, because I don't have time for it." I stared at my wife very seriously. I was nearing the end of my rope.

Stacey glared at me and curled her lips.

I could tell things were going to get worse.

"'Ridiculous'!" she screamed. "What's ridiculous is that you can even defend him after what he did to Julie. He broke her heart for what . . . some black pussy? And what do you mean, 'don't have time for it'? I know you're not talking to me like that!"

"Stacey, keep your damn voice down. Now, you know he didn't leave Julie for that—he didn't love her. What would you rather him do?—cheat on her? He didn't love Julie. Can't you understand that?"

"He should have never married her then."

"We've gone through this already, Stacey. You know why he did."

"Oh yeah, he wanted to do the right thing—please . . . 'Didn't love her'? Did he even try? While he was so busy wanting black women did he even try to love her?"

"How can you try something when it's not in your heart?"

"Now that is a ridiculous thing to say." Stacey slammed the comb down on the table. "And I'll tell you what else is ridiculous—you thinking that Vic is going to be able to come in here with his new woman, just putting her all in my face."

"In *your* face? Are you listening to yourself? Do you know how ridiculous that sounds? His coming over here has nothing to do with you. He is in love with Latrice. They are my friends. They are coming over to watch the fight, not ridicule you. You really need to get over this shit, Stacey. I mean, why are you so angry about it? Damn, you act like he killed her. You said yourself that Julie found someone new. If she's moving on, why can't you?"

"What Vic did is disgusting, Roy. He bought her a ring, he married her, and he cared for her when she lost the baby, made her feel like she was loved.

Then he just dropped her like yesterday's news. I have no respect for that. It was cowardly and cruel, and I don't want him here!"

I stood up and held on to the back of my chair. I was definitely at the end of my rope now. I took a couple of deep breaths. I looked toward the direction of our daughters' bedroom doors. I didn't like for them to hear or see us argue like this. "Listen, Stacey, because this will be the only time I say this—I am the man of this house; I pay the majority of the bills here—if I want my friends to come over, then there is not a damn thing you can say or do about it. Are we clear?"

Stacey scowled at me and stepped toward me. In a low, guttural voice she said, "Oh, I hear you. Now you hear me—if you let Vic into this house, the girls and I will leave it. Are we clear?"

Before I could say anything, Stacey turned around, grabbed the comb from the table, and stormed to the girl's bedroom.

When I heard the door slam shut, I went to the bathroom and grabbed the Tylenol from the medicine cabinet. After that, I grabbed my coat and left. I needed to cool down and think. I couldn't believe she had taken it to such an extreme. I couldn't believe she threatened to leave and take the girls with her.

"There is no way in hell that's happening," I whispered to myself. Needing some advice, I turned my cell phone on and called Colin as I got into my car.

Stacey

19

When Roy left, I did Sheila's hair and sat alone in darkness for a long while as I contemplated what I should do. I was pissed and hurt. I couldn't believe Roy stormed out the way he did. More importantly, I couldn't believe he had gone off on me. Never in all of our years together had he spoken to me that way, and I wasn't about to stand for it. Why couldn't he just understand where I was coming from?

I couldn't imagine Roy doing to me what Vic did. I felt Julie's pain, without having to go through what she did. The more I thought about it, the angrier I became. The way I looked at it, when a person said 'I do,' they just did. And anyone who wasn't willing should never have made the vow. Vic should have never used the word, and his argument about trying to do the right thing didn't fly with me. The right thing was to take care of his responsibility without stringing Julie along and allowing her to hand him her heart to break.

No one could've convinced me that what Vic did wasn't cowardly. It made him less of a man in my eyes. Of all people, I expected my husband to understand that, but no, instead he chose to side with Vic. *Fine.*

I grabbed the phone and dialed Julie's number. "Hey, girl," I said when Julie answered

"Hey, Stacey. I haven't spoken to you all week. How are you?"

"I'm good. The girls continue to drive me up the wall, and Roy is still Roy."

"And you love him for that."

I cracked a knuckle. "Mmm hmm. So, anyway, what's going on with you? Are you still talking to what's-his-name?"

"Who . . . Derrick? Oh, yes, I'm still talking to him; we've gone out several times."

"Sounds like you like him." I was happy to hear the excitement in her voice; that was nice for a change, not hearing her depressed frame of mind.

"He's nice, Stacey, really nice. And attentive. But, as you know, I'm not trying to go anywhere too soon. I'll be keeping my guard up for a while."

"Don't keep it up so high that you miss something worth keeping."

"I know, but I have to keep it up like this."

"Does he know about Vic?"

"No. Nothing's serious enough for him to know."

"Okay, I understand." I grabbed the remote and turned the TV on.

"I think he would be down with it; he's very understanding and easy to talk to."

"Sounds like he could be a real man." I flipped through the channels, not really looking for anything in particular.

Julie laughed. "Yes, he certainly is that."

I paused with my channel surfing and said, "You didn't!"

Julie laughed.

"What happened to keeping your guard up?"

"I got weak one night, and it fell."

"Any regrets?"

"At first I had some. Vic was the last man I had been intimate with."

"Too bad."

"After it happened with Derrick, I felt terrible . . . like I'd cheated or something."

"'Cheated'?"

"I still love Vic, even if he doesn't love me. Getting over him is not an easy thing for me, and even though our relationship no longer exists, I still feel tied to him in some ways."

"Well, you better untie yourself quick."

"I know. Which is why I realized that what happened with Derrick wasn't a bad thing; it was actually good for me. It helped get rid of some pent-up stress."

"I bet it did, girl."

Julie laughed again. "You are crazy!"

"Not yet," I said, thinking about Roy and our argument, "but I'm getting there."

"Huh?"

"Oh nothing, girl. Just babbling over here. So, anyway, I'm glad you're okay with what happened."

"Yeah, I am. It's a slow process, but I'm getting

over Vic. Sleeping with Derrick was a necessary step in that process, but like I said, I am keeping that wall up."

"Well, good for you." I went back to flipping through the channels and then stopped on an infomercial for a knife set. It reminded me of why I had called her. "Hey, listen, what are you doing this coming Saturday night?"

"Saturday night? I'm not doing anything special. I'll probably be with Derrick again—why?"

"Oh, we're having a get-together to watch the Mike Tyson fight. Why don't you and Derrick come over?"

"'A get-together'? That would be nice. It'd be nice to see Roy and the girls, and even Colin, with his conceited self."

"Oh, he is definitely that."

We laughed together, and then Julie said in a darker tone, "I assume Vic is going to be there."

"Yeah . . . with his friend."

There was a long moment of silence.

"'His friend'? I see."

I could hear the sadness in her voice. It was a bad idea. "Hey listen, girl, why don't we forget I ever mentioned Saturday? Why don't we just have a little girls' night out of our own?"

"We could do that some other time—Derrick and I are coming on Saturday."

"You are? You sure you're okay with Vic being here?"

"Vic threw us away, and I've got to move on."

"Good. I look forward to seeing you and Derrick, who you only tell me about in bits and pieces. I don't even know what he looks like. Is he ugly, girl? Please tell me you didn't find yourself an ugly man."

Julie laughed out loud.

I started laughing too. "I'm serious, girl."

"No, he's not ugly. I just haven't told you much about him because I want to be sure it's going somewhere. But don't worry, you'll be both surprised and pleased when you do meet him."

"Surprised and pleased, huh?"

"Yup."

"No hints?"

"Not one."

I turned the TV off and stood up. It was nearing twelve-thirty and Roy had been gone for close to two hours now. "Okay, girl. I better get my beauty sleep."

"Okay. Kiss the girls for me and say hi to Roy. Tell him I may be coming to Carmax to see him soon."

"Okay. Will do. Take care, and I'll talk to you during the week to make sure you haven't changed your mind."

"Oh, I won't change it; actually, I'm a little curious about what Vic's friend looks like."

"Don't be."

"Have you met her?"

"I will this Saturday."

"Okay. Then we can judge her together."

"Sounds like a plan," I said, looking out the window. *Where the hell is Roy?*

"Okay, bye for now, Stacey."

"Talk to you soon." I hung up the phone and smiled.

I peeked out through the window again, and

when a car sped by the house, I sighed. Roy and I had never fought like this before. I couldn't stand what was happening between us. I knew inviting Julie over was only adding fuel to the fire. Roy was not going to be happy, but then I wasn't happy either. That's why I chose my side.

I looked at the clock and then called Roy's cell phone. He didn't answer, and I didn't leave a message.

Colin

20

Emily and I were on some other level of intense ecstasy when my cell phone went off, so there was no way in hell I was about to answer it. We were conducting round two, with the help of Barry White and candle wax. We had already capped round one off with strawberry massage oil and whipped cream.

This was the fourth time we had hooked up. I never expected it to go past the first. I actually tried to convince myself that sleeping with her was only a moment of weakness on my part. I even tried to make up for the slippage by hooking up with a couple of the finest sisters I had in my book of conquests, the ones with stars beside their names. But despite the fun, I couldn't deny it—I couldn't get Emily out of my head.

Everything about her was captivating me. Being with her was cool, because I was able to keep it real. Although she was white, I soon came to realize that she was more down than any female I'd ever met, black or white. To top it off, she could match me "freak for freak" in the bedroom, which is what was going on when my cell went off. That's why I ignored it.

But when the knocking started on my front door fifteen minutes later, I couldn't help getting frustrated. When that happened, my focus got all screwed up.

I looked at Emily as she rode me. Damn, she was looking fine. I shook my head.

"Go and get rid of them," she said with a smile.

"Oh, I'll do more than get rid of them," I said, slipping into my boxers. "Vic is about to catch a beat-down." I hurried to the door and opened it. I was surprised to see that it was Roy. From the look on his face, I could tell it wasn't a social visit. "Roy? What are you doing here?"

He sighed. "Man, I need to talk. I have some issues."

I took a peek behind me toward the bedroom, where Emily was waiting in all her naked splendor. I looked back at him. Damn, he really looked like he needed to talk. But I was just beginning to hit my stride. "Yo, dog, can this wait until tomorrow? I'm kind of in the middle of something."

Without waiting for an answer, he stormed past me into my living room. "She said she'd take the damn girls, man!" he yelled. "Can you believe that shit?"

I bowed my head, closed the door, and turned around. I was as limp as a soggy noodle. It was obvious that I wasn't going to get rid of him that easily. "Roy, what the hell are you talkin' about? You're not makin' any sense."

Pacing and burning a hole in my rug, he said, "Stacey threatened to take the girls, man."

"What? What do you mean, 'threatened'? Since when have you guys been having problems like that?"

Roy continued pacing, and spoke with his hands in full swing. "Man, she's been tripping over Vic."

"Still? Are you for real?"

"Colin, she can't get over Vic leaving Julie."

I looked at him and before I could say anything, he said, "I know, I know—it doesn't make sense. I told her that, but she's not trying to hear that."

"Oh well," I said, looking back to the room, "that's her hang-up." I looked back at Roy.

He sat down on my couch. "Now, how did you go from Vic to her taking the girls?"

"Man, you know how I told you guys about coming over to watch the Tyson fight this Saturday?"

"Yeah."

"Well, when I told her that Vic was coming, and that he was going to bring Latrice, she all but had it. She went off and said she didn't want him in the house, and if he came, then she'd leave with the girls!"

I stared down at him and crossed my arms. "Come on, dog, she said that for real?"

"As real as a heart attack."

"Man, she can't be serious about that. She can't be trippin' like that, not Stacey."

Roy looked up at me and said solemnly. "She can, and is."

"Damn." I sat down beside him.

"So what do I do, man? I don't want to lose my girls, or Stacey."

I sucked my teeth and lay back on the couch. Scratching my stomach, I said, "Roy, listen, I'ma be real up front with you on this one. I know you love Stacey and your girls, but let's keep it real—if Stacey were to actually do you like that, she would be completely in the wrong. She knows she can't get away with that; she's just talkin' shit, like most women do. Stop stressin' over it. If she wants to be mad, let her be mad, but I'm tellin' you, she's talkin' shit."

- "How do you know?"

"Because she loves you, and she knows how tight we all are. In the end, when it comes down to it, she'll be by your side." I gave him dap and then stood up. "Yo, dog, go home to your wife and kids—don't sweat this."

He stood up. "Thanks, man. And I'm sorry for barging in here like this; she just had me freaked when she went off."

"It's cool," I said, opening the front door. "I'll call you tomorrow to see how things went."

"Cool, man, and I'm sorry for interrupting."

I nodded and closed the door. When I walked back into the room, Emily was under the covers, pretending to be asleep. I could tell it was fake, because I saw her eyes open a fraction.

I climbed under the covers and slid next to her. "That's why I'm never getting married—I don't want that hassle."

Emily opened her eyes and turned toward me. "So most women talk shit, huh?"

I kissed her on the lips. "Nope, not most, all women do."

She gave me a hard punch on my shoulder. "I've got you shit talking right here."

I laughed and then grabbed the blanket, pulling it above our heads. "Talk all the shit you want, girl."

Latrice

21

I had just come in from the gym when my phone rang. I threw my gym bag down and grabbed the receiver. I was expecting it to be Vic, but when I looked at the caller ID and saw it wasn't him, I thought about not answering the call. Knowing how persistent he could be, I hit the TALK button. "Hello Bernard."

"Latrice," Bernard said, "it's been a while. How have you been?"

"I've been good. And you?"

"Not bad."

"I'm surprised you called."

"I just wanted to say hi, maybe talk for a couple."

"Bernard, I don't mean to be rude, but I just got in and I'm tired." I wanted desperately to get off the phone, as old memories started to resurface, memories I didn't want to have.

"Just for a few minutes, LaLa." He called me by the pet name he'd given me long ago. "That's all I'm asking for."

I sighed. "Bernard, we can't do this. Besides, I don't think your wife would approve of us talking."

"'Wife'? When did I get married?"

"I heard through the grapevine you married Lynette this past summer."

"Well, you heard wrong; your grapevine has it all backwards—we actually broke up."

"Sorry to hear that. What happened?" I cursed myself silently for asking.

"I'm still in love with someone else."

I took a deep breath and exhaled slowly. As much as I didn't want to admit it to myself, Bernard still had a hold on me, and hearing his deep, sexy voice was not the thing I needed to hear. Nor was his last comment.

"She must be a hell of a woman, to make you end your relationship."

"Oh, she's a hell of a woman, all right."

I cleared my throat and stared at myself in the mirror. *Don't fall back girl.*

"What was that?"

I shook my head. I didn't realize I had thought out loud. *I need to get off the phone.* "Nothing. Bernard, I have to go. I have plans this evening."

"With who?"

"A friend."

"Is this a male or female friend?"

I sighed. "Bernard, does it really matter?"

"Yes, it does."

"Why?"

There was silence for a long second, which gave me enough time to think about him and how wonderful he was to me when we were together.

When we initially met, he was married and unhappy. His wife was a money-hungry, selfish bitch. From the first moment I saw them together, I thought he was too good for her triflin' ass.

It took a while before we developed into anything. I was reluctant because he was married, and I didn't want to disrespect that union. So we started doing lunch, then dinner, and eventually breakfast.

By the time that started to happen, it was obvious to the both of us that we were falling in love. That's why he finally made the decision to leave his wife. And I wasn't complaining.

Bernard gave me all the love and respect I needed to be happy forever. He pampered me in all the right ways, at all the right times. He gave himself unconditionally.

When his divorce finally went through, we already had plans established for our wedding. But then Danita died, and that changed everything.

Bernard was there for me, just like he had always been, but her death had been too hard for me. I sank into an insurmountable pool of depression, and as time went on, I found it more and more difficult to give anything to anyone. That's why he ended up in the arms of Lynette Cooper, a co-worker of his who had been eyeing him since day one.

As I pushed him away, she was readily there to accept him into the web she was spinning. Eventually, Bernard couldn't get out, and he walked out of my life. I knew I was losing a good thing by letting him go without a fight, but I couldn't do it. I needed the time away to find the will to be happy again.

Now that I had, the last thing I needed was for the man who I had never completely gotten over to come back into my life and tell me that he was once again free.

"What do you want, Bernard?"

"LaLa, I'm not going to beat around the bush with you."

"Good. Because I don't have much time."

"LaLa, I love you; I want us back."

"Bernard, you walked away from our relationship."

"LaLa, you pushed me away, you know that. I tried to be there for you in every way possible. I never wanted us to be apart. I never wanted to be with anyone else."

"You had a funny way of showing that . . . as fast as you ended up in Lynette's arms."

"That didn't happen overnight, Latrice."

"Well, it happened."

"You let it."

I sighed and massaged my temples. "Bernard, we shouldn't be talking about this." I sat on my bed and closed my eyes.

"Why?"

"Because we've both moved on."

"Have we?"

I lay back and stared up at the ceiling. "Bernard, I'm involved with someone, okay."

The volume in his voice dropped as he said, "I see. Is it real?"

"As real as it can be."

"But is it as real as what we had?"

I slammed my hand down on the mattress. I didn't need this. "Why did you call, Bernard?"

"Because I got tired of denying the truth."

"Which is?"

"That I am and always have been in love with you, and I feel we belong together."

I felt a tear snake away from the corner of my eye. *Why now?* I looked over at my clock. Vic was probably on his way over. *Damn.* "Vic—I mean, Bernard, I have to go."

"'Vic'? Is that who my competition is?"

"This is not a game, Bernard."

"Is Vic the man you're seeing?"

"Bernard, I have to go."

Before I could disconnect the call, I heard him say, "I'm going to get you back, Latrice. I'm still in love with you, and I know you feel the same."

I hit the OFF button and let the phone fall from my hand. I continued to stare at a spot on the ceiling as tears fell from my eyes.

Vic

22

I took a deep breath before I rang Roy's doorbell. He'd called me during the week and told me all about his argument with Stacey and the fact that she was still harboring ill feelings toward me. I expected that and was prepared to deal with any attitude she was going to give to Latrice, who I'd warned ahead of time. What I didn't expect was to hear how she'd threatened to leave with the girls if I came over. That surprised me, because I could never imagine Stacey being that ugly.

Once he told me about his wife's threat, I decided that I wasn't going to go. I didn't want to cause him any unnecessary drama, but Roy was adamant about me coming over.

"Vic, listen, I want to see you and Latrice here having a good time Saturday night."

"I just don't want to cause you any headache,

Roy. Latrice and I can chill at my place and watch the fight from there."

"That's not an option, Vic. I want to see you and Latrice here primed and ready to see Mike administer an ass-whupping of epic, round-one proportions."

"You sure, man? Believe me, it's no problem for me to chill at my place."

"It would be a problem for me, Vic; you're my boy. Stacey's going to have to accept that what went on with you and Julie is really none of her business."

"And what about her threat?"

"I'll deal with my wife. You just make sure you're here in time to see the preliminary fights. You know those will last longer than the main event."

"True. Okay, man, as long as you're sure, we'll be there."

"Cool. See you Saturday."

"Later."

I turned to Latrice. "You ready?"

She smiled and said, "No, the question is, are *you* ready? I don't have a problem with this woman, and if she's smart, she won't have a problem with me."

"Well, just in case she does, we're not sticking around. I'm not trying to bring you in on any mess."

"Ring that bell, Vic. I can hold my own against a nasty attitude. Won't be the first time, and it won't be the last."

I gave her a deep kiss and then rang the bell. As we waited, I couldn't help wondering what lay on the other side of the door.

"Vic," Stacey said, "how are you? Come on in."

I'm sure Stacey could read the confusion in my eyes as I stared back at her. The last thing I expected to see when the door opened was a smiling Stacey. I didn't actually speak or move until Latrice gave me a light tap in the middle of my back. "Hey, what's up, Stacey? Nice to see you. It's been a while."

"Yes, it has." Stacey looked at Latrice. "This must be the new woman I've heard so much about." She extended her hand. "I'm Stacey, Roy's wife."

Latrice took Stacey's hand and smiled. "Latrice. Nice to meet you; I've heard so much about you."

"All good things, I hope."

Latrice laughed. "Definitely interesting."

Stacey stepped to the side. "Well, come on in. It's freezing."

"Where are the girls?" I asked, disappointed they hadn't come running up to me.

"Oh, they spent the night at their friend's house and left us grown-ups alone and unsupervised for the night."

"Right, right."

Closing the door, Stacey said, "Vic, you know where to put the coats. Latrice, if you don' t mind, I could use a hand in the kitchen before the festivities start."

"No problem."

Latrice's smile was as fake a smile as I had ever seen. I could tell she didn't like Stacey. To be honest, I didn't know if I did at that particular moment either.

I took her coat and hung it up with mine and let the ladies go their way. Then I headed to the living room, where Roy was hooking up his illegal black box to the big screen. "What's up, man?" I said, taking a seat.

From behind the TV, Roy asked, "Hey, is the reception clear yet?"

"Not yet. Wait . . . now it is."

"Finally." Roy stood up. "So what's up, man?"

"You tell me. What's up with Stacey? I expected to walk into a battlefield man. Why is she being so nice?"

Roy shrugged his shoulders. "You got me. I came home yesterday and she apologized for the way she was acting. Said that everything would be okay tonight. I'm as surprised as you are. Where's Latrice?"

"She's in the kitchen with Stacey."

"Alone?"

"Yeah, but it's cool. Trice can hold her own."

"Man, I'm trying to watch a fight on TV live and in stereo, not live and in my living room."

I laughed. "Don't worry. Unless Stacey throws the first blows, it'll be cool."

"We'll see." Roy ran to the kitchen and then came back with four beers. He handed me two of them. "They're both alive . . . for now."

I took a long swallow of the Heineken. "So when's Colin getting here? And I wonder if he's bringing Emily with him? You know they've hooked up more than once, right?"

"Yeah, I know. I think I barged in on them a couple nights back when I stopped by his place. And yeah, he's bringing her. I think they might actually become a 'for-real' item some time."

"Damn! The world must be coming to an end. Who would have ever thought Colin would come close to having a real relationship?"

"With a white female at that. Man, back in Tennessee, relationships like y'all's are a rare thing to see."

"For real?"

"Oh definitely. You just don't mix like that in the South. That was one thing I had to get used to when I first moved up here. The interracial thing is like taboo in the South."

"How do you feel about it?"

"I couldn't care less. Love doesn't love anybody; the person does. And as long as the person you're with loves you back, then that's all that matters."

I held up my beer can for a toast. "I hear that."

He tapped his can against mine.

Just then, the doorbell rang. Roy stood up and said, "Must be Colin."

As they showed a clip of Mike Tyson from his glory days, I heard Colin's voice. "*Wasaaaaaap!*" he said, walking into the living room, sounding like the guys from the Budweiser commercials.

I answered back, "*Wasaaaaaabi!*"

Roy trailed a couple of seconds behind and said, "How you doin'?" in his best Italian voice.

We all laughed.

Colin said, "Yo, those commercials are the shit."

"Yeah," I said, "we need to do something like that—blow up with a catch phrase."

"Yeah," Colin said. "How about, 'Where da 'ho's at?'" He laughed and grabbed a beer.

I smiled. "You better not let Emily hear that. Speaking of which—where is she?"

"She's in the kitchen with Latrice and Stacey. And please . . . I say that around her all the time."

"Sounds like you're into her," Roy said, raising the volume for the first fight, which was about to start.

Colin sat down in my beanbag and nodded. "I can't front—Emily is cool. She keeps it real with me, and I'm able to keep it real with her."

"Uh oh," I said. "Is the player card slowly dissolving?"

Colin looked at me and raised an eyebrow. "Please, dog—I'm a player for life."

"We'll see," I said.

We all laughed and then watched as the first round of the first fight began. Two junior middleweight boxers, one a Mexican, and the other a black kid from New York, were going head to head, pounding each other with all they had. By the end of the third round, the black fighter's eye was so swollen, his trainers threw in the towel.

"Damn," I said, stuffing some chips into my mouth, "Latino fighters are some fighting-ass fools."

"Yeah," Colin added. "You remember Chavez? He was like a brick. And what about Duran and his 'hands of stone'?"

"Yeah," Roy threw in, "even the pretty boys like De La Hoya and Trinidad are tough as nails."

When the second fight, featuring Christy Martin,

was set to begin, the ladies came into the living room. Emily flopped down with Colin, and Stacey sat on Roy's lap.

I looked at Latrice as she came to sit down beside me. She gave me an "everything's-okay" look. I squeezed her hand and then, out of the corner of my eye, caught what seemed to be a glare coming from Stacey. When I turned to face her, she gave me a smile. I smiled back and then focused on the fight.

While Christy Martin was pummeling her opponent, the doorbell rang. Roy looked at his watch. It was past eleven. "You expecting company?" he asked Stacey.

Stacey didn't say a word as she got up and left the room.

I looked at Roy. "What's up?"

"No idea," he said. He got up and left also.

"Christy is no joke," Colin said.

Latrice and Emily both sucked their teeth; they were not feeling the female boxers.

As round two began, I heard a voice I hadn't expected or wanted to hear. Apparently, so did Colin, because he looked at me and then shook his head.

A few seconds later, Roy trudged into the living room. It was obvious from the look on his face that he was not happy. He didn't say a word as he sat down.

I clenched and unclenched my fist several times in a row. I looked from him to Colin. We all had the same look. I took a deep breath. I couldn't believe what was about to happen.

Latrice noticed my agitation. "What's wrong?" she asked.

I shook my head and let my breath out slowly.

"Vic," Latrice said again, "what's wrong?"

I finally opened my mouth to speak, but before I could get a word out, Stacey's voice pierced the air. "Everyone . . . look who dropped by."

Latrice

23

When Stacey announced Julie's appearance, the first thought that came to my mind, and which almost slipped from my lips, was that Stacey was a true bitch. I couldn't believe what was happening. And from the evil look on Vic's face, neither could he. I looked at Emily, whose mouth, just like Colin's, was *O*-shaped.

Emily knew all about Julie because I'd told her all of the things Vic had told me about them being together. I gave Stacey my nastiest glare, and she stared directly back at me. I was hot and ready to go ghetto on her ass.

Vic had warned me about how angry Stacey was about him dumping Julie. And after sitting with her in the kitchen, I realized her nice act had been nothing but a front.

We sat and chitchatted, while Vic and Roy were in the living room doing what guys did. We talked about things only women could love—clothes. I had on a pair of midnight-blue jeans from the Limited, and a white turtleneck. On my feet, I had on my black calf-high leather boots. Stacey had on a pair of jeans also, with a light-blue V-neck top that was just a little too tight for her top-heavy frame.

"Latrice, girl, I love those boots you have on. They are the bomb," Stacey said.

"Thanks, girl. I got them on sale at Nordstrom. Eighty bucks—can you believe it?"

"'Eighty'?—that's a steal. They still have them?"

"Uh uh, I got the last pair."

"Figures."

We talked some more about shopping, and then Stacey got personal and started talking to me about her and Roy. I knew that hearing about how they met and how long they'd been together was all part of her set-up.

Eventually, she decided to show her face by asking about me and Vic. "So how did you and Vic meet?"

"Oh, we work together."

"Oh, do you? You work together—imagine that."

I was sure she knew because, from what Vic told me, Roy shared everything with her, and I knew Roy knew the details about us. I pretended to be ignorant.

"Well, we work in different departments. We were friends for a while, and then we eventually got together."

"I see."

She was about to delve for more information when the doorbell rang.

I was glad when Roy and Emily appeared in the kitchen. "Hey, girl," I said to Emily, "I was wondering when you would get here."

"What's up, Latrice?" Emily said. "Yeah, we had some things to take care of before we left his place." Emily looked at me and winked.

I shook my head.

Roy looked at Stacey. "Baby, this is Emily; Emily, this is my wife, Stacey."

Taking Emily's hand, Stacey said, "It's nice to finally meet the woman who's managing to keep a leash around Colin's neck."

Emily laughed. "I'm trying."

Stacey looked at me. "I didn't realize you two knew each other."

I nodded. "Yeah, Emily is my girl."

"Wow!" Stacey said with another wide smile. "Imagine that! You two are best friends dating best friends."

We all laughed, but I could hear the hidden message. I knew what her game was and what type of sister she was. I just never expected her to play the hand that she did.

No one said a word as Julie smiled and stood beside her date—a tall, good-looking brother.

I gave Stacey a cross look, and she looked back at me with a smirk of her own. She was enjoying every minute of silence that hovered in the room.

I took a deep breath and held it. I was getting hot with anger. My claws were ready for some serious work.

Emily, knowing how I could get, was quick to try and diffuse my bomb. "Latrice," she said softly, touching my arm.

I looked at her and didn't say a word.

"I need to get something from the car. Can you help me with it?"

We walked out without saying a word to anybody.

Roy

24

How I didn't go off when I saw Julie walking through my door was amazing to me, but how I managed to keep from going ballistic when Stacey looked at me and smiled was even more incredible. I was so mad and so shocked, I couldn't say anything. I just nodded to Julie and her date and then went into the living room. And while everyone tried to figure out what the hell was going on, I breathed, stared at the television, and pondered about the best way to handle the situation.

My first thought was to kick Julie out of my house. I couldn't believe she had shown up like that. Worse yet, I couldn't believe Stacey had invited her over. Now I understood why she had been so damn nice.

As I sat and thought about what was going on, I glanced at Vic from the corner of my eye. He looked like he was about to hurt somebody. I could've only imagined what Latrice was feeling. I saw the disgust in her eyes when she and Emily walked outside.

Damn. Never in a million years would I have

thought Stacey capable of doing something as devious as what she did. Not my wife. Never. That's why I grabbed her arm and took her upstairs. I wanted an explanation.

Latrice

25

"**N**o, those bitches didn't go there!" I yelled as we stepped outside. *I* didn't care who heard me. I raised my voice a notch higher. "Are they crazy? They just don't know, Emily. I am not afraid to kick a bitch's ass. Oooh, girl . . ."

Emily stood safely to the side while I paced back and forth, clenching and unclenching my hands.

"I wasn't raised in no damn suburbs, Em. I will go ghetto. Oh no . . . did you see the look on Stacey's face, standing there with her simple ass? And Julie—like her shit don't stink. Emily, don't let me go to jail tonight."

Emily exhaled and shook her head. "I don't know, Latrice. I'm about to go to jail myself. That was some foul shit they just pulled."

I exhaled and shook anger from my fingertips. I paced again and breathed deeply in and out several times. I had to get myself together. I didn't want Vic to see me in all my glory. Besides, that's exactly what Stacey and Julie wanted—my ignorant side to come out. I stopped walking and faced Emily, who looked at me with concern in her eyes.

"I can't give them the satisfaction, Em,'" I said, lowering my voice. "I can't let those bitches make me come out my face."

"I can."

I shook my head and furiously passed my tongue back and forth over my teeth. "We can't go there, girl. You don't want Colin to see that, and I don't want Vic to see that."

"Colin wouldn't care."

"Well, I don't want Vic seeing that."

"So what are you going to do then? Poor Vic, he was just sitting there, not saying a word. I can imagine how he's feeling."

"Poor Vic is fuming right now," I said. "I could feel the heat coming from him. He's about to blow. Girl, if that happens—come on, let's get inside."

"Latrice, what are you going to do?"

I passed my hand through my braids and closed my eyes and counted to ten. When I finished, I turned to Emily. "Come on, girl. I'm going to finish the game Stacey and Julie started."

Colin

26

I don't know how Vic managed to keep his cool because I know I damn sure wouldn't have been able to keep mine. I was almost ready to snap when I heard Julie's voice. I could only imagine what Vic was thinking. And then there was Latrice. I was glad Emily had sense enough to get her outside before she went off. But Vic . . . his time clock was about to expire.

Stacey shocked the hell out of me. I always knew women were capable of devious shit, but I never put her in the same category. She always seemed, like she wasn't a woman. Even when she started tripping early on about Vic and Julie, I still kept her out of the "bitches and 'ho's" category I lumped most women into. But after this, her picture was entered into the database, captioned in bold—*Number One Bitch.*

I was glad when Roy pulled her upstairs, because I didn't want to see her. But having her out of the immediate picture didn't help much—Julie was still there, with as smug a look as I'd ever seen on her. She was definitely enjoying the tension, which had gotten so thick, you could cut it with a knife.

For the first time in forever, I didn't know what to do, hence the reason for my silence. But the more I watched Vic's cheeks redden and his eyes get smaller, the more I knew I had to get him out of there. I decided to follow Emily's lead. "Yo, dog"—I looked at Vic—"can you help me get some more beers and chips?" I grabbed his arm and led the way.

Latrice

27

Emily and I walked in just in time to see Colin and Vic go to the kitchen. That was good, because it left me free to play my game without having to worry about Vic interfering. I gave an indignant look to Julie as I stepped back into the living room.

She glared back at me.

Oh, it was on, and I would be damned if I was going to lose. I stepped up to her and extended my hand. She took it with a forced smile, which was obviously for her date's benefit. By the confused look on his face, I could see that he was clueless about what was going on.

"Hi," I said, applying a slight amount of pressure. "I'm Latrice." I smiled and kept my eyes locked on hers. My grip remained tight. Although she refused to look away, I could tell she was getting nervous. Silly bitch had no idea who she was dealing with.

With a half-smile, Julie said, "Hello, Latrice."

We both knew the deal, our eyes locked on one another.

I put on a straight smile and averted my attention to her date. I finally let go of Julie's hand and extended mine to him. "And you are?"

"Derrick," he replied.

As we shook hands, banging could be heard coming from upstairs. I looked at Derrick and smiled. *Poor guy*, I thought. "Nice to meet you. I'm Latrice, and this is Emily."

Derrick nodded to Emily, who stood two steps to my left. Her eyes were locked on Julie.

"Well, since everyone else has disappeared, why don't we sit down and enjoy the fights like we came to do?"

I stepped to the side and let Julie and Derrick walk by to take a seat on the couch. My heart was beating heavily. I had to pat myself on the back. I was putting on a good act . . . because all I really wanted to do was slap Julie. I sat down on the arm of the sofa. "So . . . Julie and Dirk," I said, as another preliminary bout started, "you two make a nice couple."

Derrick laughed and said quickly, "It's *Derrick*."

"Oh, I'm sorry." I pretended to have genuinely gotten his name wrong. "I'm terrible with names. Please, forgive me."

He smiled. "Happens all the time."

From a beanbag to the side, Emily snickered.

"So," I said, fixing my eyes on Julie, "how long have you guys been dating?"

Derrick opened his mouth to answer, but before he could, Julie cut in. "Oh, we're not really dating, we're just friends."

I kept my fake smile plastered on Derrick as he looked at Julie from the corner of his eye. The status of their "friendship" was obviously news to him.

"Oh, that's nice," I said. "At least you don't have to deal with the hassle of a relationship; that can be a pain sometimes—you know how men can be." I tapped Julie's leg a little harder than I needed to.

She started to open her mouth, but as Derrick chuckled, she changed her mind.

I laughed with him. I was having a good old time. "No offense to you, Darren."

He smiled back. "None taken—and it's *Derrick*."

I put my hand to my mouth. "I'm sorry. I'll get it. I promise."

From the beanbag, Emily snickered again.

"Is something wrong?" Julie snapped, looking at her.

Emily snapped her head back and gave Julie an "I-know-you-didn't" look.

Before Emily could answer, I said, "She's laughing because being in a relationship with Colin, she knows exactly how men can be sometimes. I must say, being with Vic, I know too . . . although, I wouldn't trade my relationship with him for anything." I smiled at Julie.

Derrick asked, "How long have you and Vic been together?"

I beamed at him for giving me my next round of ammunition. "You know, I don't remember. Sometimes it almost seems like forever. I can't even remember who I was with before him, and he never mentions his ex's name. I guess we were so made for each other that the length of time is insignificant."

Derrick, the innocent bystander that he was, nodded his head like he understood exactly where I was coming from.

I know Julie did, because she stared fiercely at me through slit eyes. I smiled at her.

We had all come to see the main event, but this night, Mike Tyson had to take a back seat.

Roy

28

"What the hell has gotten into you, Stacey? What kind of games are you playing?"

She looked at me with beady eyes.

"I told you I didn't want Vic in this house."

I slammed my palm down on our dressing table, causing one of our wedding pictures to fall. "Damn it! We have been through this. Whatever problems he and Julie had are their problems. Do you understand that?—theirs, not yours or mine."

"I don't care if it is their problem. I still don't want him here. Having Colin here, who disrespects women the way he does, is bad enough, but what Vic did was pathetic!"

"Damn, Stacey! He didn't love Julie. What the hell is so wrong with that? You know what?—forget it. I don't want to hear your answer. Just tell me why you called Julie. I can't believe you were that dirty."

"'Dirty'? How is inviting my friend over dirty?"

"Don't play games, Stacey. You knew Vic was

going to be here. You knew what you were setting up. Did Julie know he was going to be here?" I glared at her.

"Yes."

"Damn! Then she's just as much of a bitch as you are."

Stacey looked at me with bug eyes and an open mouth. "I can't believe you just called me a bitch."

"Believe it!" I yelled, "because only a bitch would disrespect her husband the way you just did downstairs."

"'Disrespect'? Don't you even go there. You better be the last one talking about disrespect. Even after I asked you, you didn't find it necessary to respect me and keep Vic out of this house."

Slamming my hand down again, I yelled, "Vic is my friend!"

"And Julie is mine!"

Stacey and I stared at each other. *If she were a man*—I shook my head to get rid of that thought. I turned away from her and intertwined my hands above my head. With my back to her, I said, "I can't believe you did this. I can't believe you actually did this. I would never have expected such a low act from you. You're not the woman I married. The woman I married wouldn't do something so-so—"

"The man I married would never have chosen his friends over his wife."

I opened my mouth to reply but changed my mind. It would have been pointless. Instead, in a raspy voice, I said, "I want Julie and her date out of here, Stacey. I want them both gone before I go back downstairs."

"Julie is not going anywhere. She is my friend, and I live here too."

"Let's not play any more games, Stacey. Just get Julie out of here."

"Or what . . . ?"

I exhaled and turned to face her. "Goddamn it! I'm tired of this bullshit! I said I want Julie and that muthafucka out of here! Now, I'm giving you the opportunity to get them out before things get uglier than they already are. I suggest you do that."

"Fuck you, Roy!"

I paused and glared at her. "Fuck me? No, how about fuck *you*! And while you're fucking yourself, you can get the hell out of the house too."

"You can't kick me out, I live here!"

"Fine. Then I'll leave. I've had it with this petty shit!" I moved past her and opened the door.

Before I walked away, she screamed, "Go to hell, Roy!"

I kept my back to her as I said, "I'm leaving hell right now." I slammed the door then and left my house without saying a word to anyone.

Colin

29

Vic and I looked at each other as we heard the front door slam.

"What the hell is Stacey's problem?" Vic said through clenched teeth. "Doesn't she care that she's putting her marriage in jeopardy? Is she that pressed?"

I sighed, moved to the refrigerator and grabbed two beers. As the door was closing, I thought about grabbing one for Derrick, but then I just let it close—two tears in a bucket. I twisted the bottle tops off and handed one to Vic, whose hands were noticeably shaking.

I shook my head and took a much-needed sip. "You all right, man?" I asked, feeling like that was the dumbest question. Damn, I felt bad for him.

Vic put his elbows on the kitchen counter and massaged his temples. "If Roy weren't my boy—"

"Yeah, that kept me from cursing Stacey's ass out, too."

Vic slammed his fist on the counter. "I can't believe Julie and Stacey pulled this stunt. I just can't believe it. I mean, who the fuck do they think they are?—Stacey, with her fucking smile, just loving the drama, and Julie, standing there beside that muthafucka, like there aren't any problems. Did you see him? Where the hell did she find him? And since when did she date black men?"

I stood beside him and shrugged my shoulders.

"She walked in here like she was the shit, Colin."

"I know, man; I was there."

Vic took an angry swallow of beer and slammed the bottle onto the counter. He was definitely ticking and ready to explode. I could tell by the vein pulsating in his neck that he needed to get away from the drama. Hell, we all did.

"Dog, I don't know what is going through Stacey's head, but for real, the best thing for us to do right now would be to leave."

Vic looked at me. "Who the fuck is that guy?"

"Come on, man," I said, downing my beer, "why are you trippin' over him? He don't mean shit."

"Man, I just want to know who the hell he is."

"Why? You're with Latrice. What do you care who he is? He's nobody. Shit, I feel bad for the brother. You could tell by the look on his face that he has no clue what Julie got him into."

"I wonder where the hell she met him," Vic whispered.

I shook my head. "Forget about him already. Don't start gettin' all jealous and shit. You let her go. Now, we need to go."

"Man, I need to talk to Julie first. I need to clear this shit up."

As he started to make a move to leave the kitchen, I grabbed his arm. "Yo, dog, let's grab the ladies and go." I looked at him hard to make sure he knew I wasn't going to take no for an answer.

He shook his head. "I just need to get some shit off my chest first, man."

I closed my fingers tighter around his arm. "No, you don't. The only thing you need to do is grab Latrice before she goes ballistic, and walk out of the door. Vic, I don't care if you never take my advice again, but you're taking it this time." I tightened my grip and locked eyes with his. "Roy will settle shit with Stacey."

"But Julie—"

"To hell with Julie—you don't need any more drama, man—let's go."

Reluctantly, Vic nodded and pulled away from me. He went to the sink and turned on the faucet, splashed cold water over his face and on his head. He did this a few times then turned the faucet off and grabbed a kitchen towel.

"If Roy weren't my boy—"

"Man, let's give Roy the privacy he needs, and the four of us can go somewhere and try to make something out of this disaster."

"Only because Latrice is here will I take your advice; I don't want her to see me get ignorant."

I put out my hand for some dap.

He touched his fist with mine, and then we left the kitchen. As we stepped into the living room, Latrice and Emily turned to face us. Emily gave me a look.

I nodded to let her know everything was under control, but I could still hear Vic's clock ticking. I made a motion with my head, indicating it was time to leave, and Emily came and stood beside me. I watched in nervous silence as Latrice, who hadn't risen, bent down toward Julie's ear. I couldn't help wondering if she was going to bite it like Tyson did to Holyfield. That would have been some ugly shit.

Mercifully, all she did was whisper something.

My eyes were focused on Julie the whole time. I could tell from her reaction that she didn't like whatever it was that was said.

Latrice smiled at Derrick. "It was a pleasure meeting you . . . Derrick."

I breathed a sigh of relief when she got up without another word and came to stand beside Vic. Nothing else needed to be said, so we all left.

As I closed the door, I could hear Derrick ask, "What happened?"

When we got to our cars, we all turned to Latrice. We all asked the same question with our eyes.

"What?" Latrice asked.

"What did you tell her?" Vic asked.

Latrice smiled. "Tell who?"

"Come on, Trice," Emily said.

Finally I spoke out. "Don't leave us hangin'. I saw Julie's reaction. Whatever it was that you said, she didn't like it."

Latrice laughed and turned to Vic. "You know, only because I have respect for you did I not kick that bitch's ass. And I made sure to tell her that. But I'm letting you know now, the next time she or Stacey pull some shit like this—"

Before she could finish, a voice spoke out from behind us. "There won't be a next time."

We all turned around as Roy stepped out of the shadows.

"My nigga," I said, moving toward him, "I thought you were gone."

"Nah, I just had to get out of the house to clear my head." He turned to Vic and Latrice. "Guys, I am sorry about what went down. Believe me, I had no idea that was going to happen. Vic, you know I wouldn't set you up like that."

Vic nodded his head. "It's cool, man. No need to apologize. I know this wasn't your doing. I just can't believe Stacey showed her face like that. I mean, I know she's your wife . . ."

Roy shrugged his shoulders. "I feel the same way."

We were all quiet then. The night was supposed to have been chill, and instead, here we all were, bummed out. It had to change.

I said, "Yo, it's a Saturday night, and it's still early. Why let it go to waste? Why don't we all head to Jillian's, have a couple of drinks, play some pool, and catch the highlights of the fight on one of the big screens."

Emily squeezed my hand. "That's a good idea."

"Yeah," Latrice said. "I could use a Bloody Mary right about now. Vic?"

Vic, still visibly shaken after seeing Julie and her date, nodded. No matter how happy he was with Latrice, seeing Derrick was still a subtle blow to his ego.

Shit, seeing any man with your ex was a blow.

I looked at Roy. He too had gone through a rough night. Julie and Stacey had really shown some ugly sides. "You down, dog?"

Roy turned and looked back toward his house. He stared silently for a few seconds before he answered in a defeated tone. "Yeah, I'm down."

We all left then, and had a better night than we anticipated. We drank, laughed, watched highlights of Iron Mike landing a knockout blow, and then went home.

I stayed at Emily's place, and gave Roy my house keys. He wanted to be alone, as did Emily and I.

Julie

30

Up until I saw Vic, I had been doing okay. While it wasn't easy, I'd finally gotten to a point where I accepted life without him. But when I saw him with Latrice, my restructured heart shattered all over again, and the pain resurfaced. I knew that he would be there with her, and I thought I was going to be able to get through the evening without letting anything bother me. But that wasn't possible. I may have found a way to keep my composure and appear fine on the outside for everyone's benefit, but on the inside I was an emotional wreck.

The moment I saw him, I regretted my decision to be there. I went from moving forward to moving backward as I longed to be in his arms again. Even though Derrick was there with me, if Vic had been alone, I probably would have tried to talk to him and convince him that leaving me was a mistake.

When Latrice whispered her threat in my ear

before she walked away, the only thing that kept me from snapping back with a warning of my own was Vic's eyes, which were locked on mine. I'd never seen him look so angry and volatile. As slim as my chances of winning him back were, I knew that saying anything to Latrice at that point would have definitely hammered the final nail into the coffin, a coffin that I prayed was still open, despite Vic's venomous glare.

After that night, I decided to make one last effort to try and change his mind. I went to his job, instead of trying to call. I wanted to talk to him face to face and make him understand that we belonged together.

"What do you want, Julie?" Vic asked as he approached me. He'd had me waiting in the lobby for fifteen minutes after the guard at the front called and told him I was downstairs.

I didn't care about the wait; I had a purpose. "Hello to you too, Vic. I came to talk."

Vic frowned and folded his arms across his chest. "I don't have time, Julie; I'm busy."

I stepped to him and put my hand on his arm. In a soft voice, I said, "Please, Vic . . . just give me a few minutes."

Vic glared at me, and for a second I didn't think he'd give in.

"Ten minutes."

We walked outside and sat at an empty picnic table. Actually, I sat. He stood, obviously letting me know he had no intention of getting comfortable.

"Vic—"

"What you did was childish."

"What are you talking about?"

"Don't play games, Julie. You and Stacey knew I'd be there with Latrice—that's the only reason why you and your *friend* showed up." He glared down at me.

Feigning ignorance was not going to work. "I miss you, Vic," I said, honestly. "You're right—I did know you were going to be there with Latrice. Yes, that's why I came—I just wanted to see you. And I wanted to see who you replaced me with."

"Julie, I didn't replace you with anybody; I ended our marriage because I wasn't happy."

As hard as I tried to fight them, tears began falling from my eyes. "Vic, I love you."

"Julie, don't—"

"Don't what?" I shouted. "Don't tell you how much you mean to me, and how happy I wanted to make you? Don't tell you that I've never loved any man the way I loved you, and that I never want to love that way again?"

"Keep your voice down, Julie." Vic looked around at several employees who'd been out smoking.

I didn't care about the audience though. My tears were falling, and my anger and frustration were rising. I slammed my hand down on the table. "You fuckin' hurt me, Vic! I did nothing to deserve the shit you've put me through. The shit you're *still* putting me through. Why are you doing this to me?—can you tell me that, please? You said that you loved me. Is this how you treat someone you love?"

Vic's face reddened with embarrassment as a few female co-workers sucked their teeth and shook their heads in disapproval. He'd always hated to have anyone in his business, but I didn't give a shit. They could have pulled up a chair and taken notes for all I cared. I'd been holding my pain inside for so long that I quickly forgot all about wanting to talk.

"I hope your little romance with your bitch blows up in your face, Vic. I hope you get to experience the pain I'm feeling."

"Julie—goddamn—why can't you just understand that I did this to avoid hurting you in a worse way? Yes, I loved you, but I wasn't in love with you. I wasn't happy. You deserve to be with someone who wants to make you happy, someone who wants to be your everything. I'm sorry, but I'm not that guy."

I twisted my mouth. "Well, thank you for being such a stand-up guy," I spat sarcastically.

Vic shook his head and frowned, only making me angrier.

"Doesn't it matter to you that you've put me through this? Are you that damn cold?"

"Look, Julie, I'm sorry that you're hurting. Whether you want to believe this or not, I don't take pleasure in your pain. Leaving was just something that I had to do."

Had to do? I stood up, not caring about the people who stood around to enjoy the show. I walked over to Vic, who was obviously uncomfortable with the attention. "Go to hell, Vic"—I slapped him hard across the face—"you and that bitch!" I slapped him again, harder this time, and then stormed away.

I wasn't finished. With my hopes all but dead and buried, I wanted revenge of some kind. Revenge for the betrayal and abandonment Vic had heaped on me. Seething in my car, I drove around the company's parking lot until I found Vic's car. I shut off the engine, pulled my keys from the ignition, and approached his Eclipse. I didn't care who saw me as I scratched a message across the trunk, doors, and hood.

"Sorry, Vic," I said out loud, "it was just something I had to do."

Vic

31

Angry wouldn't have been the right word to describe how I felt when I saw what Julie had done to my car. Pissed off wouldn't have even worked. I needed seven words to explain what I was feeling inside as I stood with my hands balled up, while my fellow co-workers walked to their cars, some snickering and others gasping—I was about to go to jail.

I walked around my car and growled at the messages left and the four tires that were slashed. I slammed my fist down on the hood. "Goddamn!"

Just then Roy and Colin pulled up. I'd called them to come and pick me up.

"Oh shit," Colin said, barely stifling a laugh.

"Damn, man," Roy added.

They walked around the car, surveying the damage.

"You are a fucking asshole . . . I hate you . . . go to hell, you pathetic dog." Colin looked at me after he finished his oral presentation. "Damn, man, I didn't think Julie was capable of some shit like this."

"Neither did I," Roy added.

I slammed my hand on the hood again. "She's not going to get away with this shit." I looked at Colin. "Man, take me over to her house."

"For what?"

"Man, if she thinks she can fuck up my car and embarrass me at my job like this and get away with it, then—"

"Then what?" Colin asked. "What you gonna do, dog?—beat her ass?"

I kicked my flat tire. "Maybe."

"Shut up, Vic," Colin said. "You know you ain't kickin' no woman's ass, so stop talkin' shit. Dog, she fucked up your shit—that's what women do when they're angry and hurting."

Roy shook his head. "He's right, man. At least you can get the car repaired."

"So what . . . you guys saying that I'm just supposed to let this go, let her get away with this?"

Colin put his arm around my shoulder. "Dog, that's exactly what I'm sayin'—chalk this one up to experience. She got this round, but you got Latrice and your happiness. Leave it at that. Throw in the towel and go home with your black eye. Besides, you really don't want to roll to her house and leave your shit here. You've had enough people drive by to inspect the damage. Just call a tow truck and have them come and pick it up. Take it directly to the body shop."

I looked at Colin and then Roy, who nodded in agreement. Then I looked at my car. "Doesn't she understand that I would have hurt her more if I'd stayed with her?"

"No, dog," Colin answered. "She's a woman scorned . . . and she loved your ass. Like I said, throw in the towel and go home. Now call the tow truck. I'm gettin' tired of seeing all these people drive by."

I sighed as I grabbed my cell phone and called AAA. I don't know how I did it, but I managed to not call Julie.

I got my car back two weeks later.

Roy

32

"**D**addy!"
I smiled as my little girls climbed into the car and hugged and kissed me. "Hey, you two! How are my little angels doing?"

"We're fine!" they said in unison.

"Are we going to McDonald's?" Jenea asked.

"Yeah, can we, Daddy . . . please?" Sheila begged.

I looked at my twin daughters with a very serious face and said, "Are you two crazy? McDonald's? You want me to take you there and pass up on the broccoli and lima beans?"

"Yes!" they yelled as they buckled their seat belt.

"Lima beans are yucky!" Sheila said, making a scrunched-up face.

Jenea followed with her own, "Ewww!"

I laughed and pulled away from the curb. I didn't even wave at Stacey as she stood by the front door.

* * *

We had been separated for four months. The breakup of our marriage happened just a couple of days after the fiasco at the house. After the heated argument we had, I decided to stay by Colin for two nights. I needed that time to cool off and gather my thoughts. I wanted to make sure that when I did go back home to deal with Stacey, I would be in the right frame of mind. I didn't want another confrontation like the one we'd had. Stacey may have disrespected me, but I had crossed the line when I called her a bitch. I had never called her out of her name like that, and I regretted doing so.

When I finally did go back home, I had every intention of apologizing for that and trying to get us back on track. The last thing I expected was to end up walking back out of the house with the realization that my marriage wasn't going to last.

"So what . . . did you forget you had a family?"

I had just walked through the front door, and it had taken me a good five minutes just to do that. I looked at Stacey and sighed. She had become so ugly in such a short amount of time. "Hello to you, too," I said, closing the door behind me.

"Don't give me a hello—you stormed out of here and embarrassed the hell out of me in front of Julie and Derrick."

"You embarrassed me in front of my friends," I said, struggling to keep my voice down. I knew the girls were sleeping. Although I had called them during my time away, I had missed them like crazy.

"I don't care about your friends," Stacey hissed.

I stared hard at her. Her eyes, normally soft and

sparkling, were void of any expression, except malice. Her lips, normally kissable, were curled into a snarl. "Well that's good, because I don't give a shit about your friends either, Stacey." I inhaled and exhaled after I said that because I knew a dark cloud was about to form in our living room. Accompanying the clouds would be a few bolts of lightning.

"Go to hell, Roy!"

"I am standing right in it," I yelled, no longer able to keep my cool.

"Then leave!"

"'Leave'? I did that already. But you know what, I pay the bills here. If anyone should leave, it should be you."

"Oh, no, you are not kicking me and the girls out like that."

"Who the hell said anything about the girls?—they have no problem with my friends; that's your hang-up."

"'Hang-up'?" She crossed her arms defiantly.

I crossed mine also. "That's right—hang-up. You're destroying our marriage over other people's problems—that is sad."

"'Destroying'? All I asked was that you respect me and not have him come around. You know how I felt about what he did."

"Why? Why, Stacey? What the hell was so bad about it? He was a man about what he did. He should be commended for that. It was better than cheating."

"'Commended' . . . for what?—finding a way out?"

"How can you look at it as a way out? If he didn't

love her, why should he waste their time? But if you want to look at it as finding a way out, you go right ahead. At least he found a way out for both of them, because if he had stayed, they would've both been unhappy."

"Unhappy, my ass—Julie is unhappy now that he found his way out."

"She didn't look so unhappy when she was conspiring with you."

"'Conspiring'? Julie is my friend; I invited her over."

"Without telling me."

"What . . .? I need your permission? I am a woman, not your child!"

"I'm not calling you a child, Stacey. You should have discussed it with me first, and you know that. I gave you that much respect when I told you Vic was coming."

"No, you disrespected me by not honoring my wishes."

I turned away from her and kicked the side of the couch. She was getting me worked up in a way I hadn't been in a long time. With my back to her, I said, "How could you do what you did, Stacey? I mean, cut the bullshit. How could you have been so conniving? I'm your husband. I love, provide, and take care of you and the girls. Even if you were mad, how could you do what you did to me?"

"I didn't want Vic here—don't you understand that?"

I turned around. "No! That's my point—I don't understand. Do you love me? Because if you love me, you have a hell of a way of showing it." I watched her and clenched my jaws.

She stood staring at me with cold eyes, eyes that I had never seen before.

"How do you do that to someone you love?"

Stacey stood before me, not moving or saying a word.

I closed my eyes and tilted my head back. When I finally brought my head down and opened my eyes again, I saw something I hadn't seen in a long time. "Why are you crying?"

After that question, what initially started out as a few teardrops quickly turned into a flood.

I moved toward her. "What's wrong, Stacey?" I hated to see her cry. I hated that our argument had escalated to the level it had. I tried to put my arms around her.

She put up her hands. "Stay away from me, Roy," she said through her tears.

"Stay away from you? You act like I was going to do something to you. I'm your husband. Stacey, I don't want us to argue like this, and I don't want you to cry. I love you. I want us to find a way to work this problem out." I moved toward her again.

This time she stepped back and stared at me. Her eyes were red and swollen from her tears.

"Let's do this together, baby," I said, pleading with my own eyes.

She shook her head. "We can't."

"What do you mean, 'we can't'? We can do anything together." I watched her as more tears fell from her eyes. I stood confused about the pain I could see she was in, but couldn't quite understand. "Stacey, please talk to me." I wanted to reach out and wrap her in my arms and somehow make her understand that together we could overcome any obstacle, but as she stood silent and un-moving, I found myself doubting that.

Finally, after seconds of tense silence crept by, Stacey, her bottom lip quivering, said, "I don't know if I can, Roy."

"What do you mean? Tell me what the problem is."

Crying uncontrollably now, she said, "I don't know if I can do this anymore."

"I don't want to argue anymore either."

"No, Roy. I mean, I-I-I don't know if I can do *us* anymore."

"What? What are you saying?" My voice was barely a whisper as I studied her.

Staring back at me with a serious gaze, she said, "I'm-I'm not sure of my feelings anymore, Roy. I need space and time to think about things."

Space and time? "'Space and time'? Where the hell is this coming from?"

"Look, Roy," she said as she looked away, "I just don't know what I want anymore, okay. I need time—can't you understand that?"

"No, I can't!" I yelled. "This just doesn't make sense to me."

"Roy, I'm only trying to do the right thing . . . like Vic. I should be commended for this," she said sarcastically.

I kicked a hole in the wall when she said that. "Commended? This is bullshit, Stacey, straight-up bullshit!"

Without responding, she ran past me and went upstairs. Left me standing alone in the living room. *She needed time?* I tried to figure out what happened between us. Where did we go wrong?

What had I done? But the more I thought about it, the more frustrated I became.

I went up to talk to her, but she kept the bedroom door locked and wouldn't let me in. I left then and went back by Colin's. I didn't talk when he opened his door.

Thankfully, he didn't press me.

I just needed to think. I fell asleep on his couch somewhere in-between my thoughts.

The next evening, I went back home, and instead of seeing Stacey or my little girls, a note met me saying, she had gone to her mother's back in Tennessee.

When I called, her mother, a woman who had become a second mother to me, answered the phone.

"Hello, Mrs. Bolton," I said into the phone.

I expected a chilly reception, because she and Stacey were like best friends and I figured Stacey had only said negative things about me.

"Hello, Roy," she kindly replied.

"How are you doing? It's been a while."

"I'm doing just fine. How are you holding up?"

I sighed. "I've been better."

"Roy, I want you to remember that when times are at their roughest, those are the times when you must keep the faith."

A tear fell from my eye when she said that. "I have to be honest, Mrs. Bolton—I don't have much faith right now."

"Roy, I don't know what is going through my daughter's head, I really don't. I've tried to talk to her, but for whatever reason, she won't open up to me. I know this is hard, but please try to hold on. Give her time; she'll come around."

I sighed again and massaged the back of my neck. "I'll try. Is she around? I'd like to speak to her."

There was a moment of silence.

"I'm sorry, Roy, but she doesn't want to talk to you. I wish I could make her, but you know how she is."

I bit down on my lip. "Okay, Mrs. Bolton, just tell her I called."

"I will."

"How are the girls?"

"They're fine. They're both sleeping right now. They know you two are having problems, so when you speak to them, be honest and answer their questions truthfully. Don't sugarcoat anything for them."

"I won't," I said, exhaling. "Can you tell them I miss them?"

"I will. And, Roy, they miss you too, and so do I. Please remember that no matter what happens between you two, you will always be my son-in-law. You've done right by my daughter—I know that, and I am thankful."

"Thank you, Mrs. Bolton. I would be proud to continue to call you my mother-in-law."

I hung up the phone and cried. I missed my family; I missed my old life. Nothing was the same anymore, and it was painful.

I didn't hear from Stacey for the next week, until she came home—without the girls. I didn't mind, because I didn't want them around to see what was happening between us.

Stacey and I screamed, cursed, and broke things. We did everything but become violent with one another. When everything was all said and done, I left the house again, only, this time I had no intention of going back.

Stacey and I officially separated six weeks later. The judge granted me alternating weekends with Jenea and Sheila—something I wasn't happy with, but would accept for the time being . . . at least until it was time to file for divorce.

When that time came, I was going to fight for full custody. I wanted the girls with me. The time wasn't coming fast enough for me, though. It all but came to a standstill during the holiday season; that was rough for me and the girls. For the first time, we didn't have our traditional family Christmas. They spent the first half of the day opening their presents with Stacey, and the other half with me.

Seeing the forced smiles on their faces was incredibly painful. They didn't enjoy Christmas like they normally did, and that made me even angrier inside . . . because they were suffering and it wasn't their fault. That Christmas Day was a long and stressful one. For New Year's, I let them stay with Stacey.

Four months had now passed as I guided my Volvo wagon down Route 1, with the girls sitting in the back.

"Okay, okay," I said playing their favorite CD— *NSYNC.* "McDonald's it is."

"Yay!" my girls cried out in unison.

I smiled on the outside and cried on the inside. I knew that they were hurting over what was happening, but they were intelligent and were actually dealing with it better than I ever would have expected. I just wished I never had to answer questions like, "When are you coming home, Daddy?" or "When are you and Mommy going to stop fighting?"

I drove the car with those questions repeating in my head. I hated having to tell them the truth. "Mommy and I aren't getting back together."

Stacey

33

A s Roy drove off with the girls, I closed the door and sighed. Even though I couldn't blame him for feeling the way he felt, it was still hurtful to see how much animosity he had toward me. He was so unlike the person that he used to be. He had become cold and bitter. Of course, I expected that, once I told him the news about not wanting to be married anymore. I wanted to tell him years ago that I didn't love him the way he loved me, but I lost the nerve after he'd proposed. That day changed my life.

It was at his mother's house, in front of his entire family on Christmas Day. We were there for dinner, since we had spent breakfast and lunch by my mother's. It was a normal celebration, filled with food and laughter—until Roy stood up and tapped his wineglass with the back of his knife. Asking for complete silence, he turned to me.

I'll never forget the silence that overtook the room. And I will always remember the feel of the spotlight that only I could see.

Right there in front of all of the stares and smiles, Roy got down on one knee, took my hand in his, and removed a ring box from his pocket.

Everyone gasped when the box was opened, revealing a beautiful, pear-shaped ring.

I felt my heart drop.

Just the night before, I had been with my true love—Rashad. And I promised him that after the holidays were over, I was going to leave Roy to be with him, because I was truly in love with him.

We had been seeing each other for a little over a year. He was the man of my dreams. We'd met at a fundraiser on campus and hit it off immediately. He did for me what Roy never really did—he made my knees weak, he made my skin tingle.

I never felt that with Roy. But I did care about him and his family, who I had become close to during the course of our relationship. And because I was so close to them, and they accepted me as one of their own, I never had the courage to end the relationship. I knew that would hurt him, and in turn, everyone else. I didn't want that. I didn't want to be the bad guy. So instead of doing what I should have done, I stayed with Roy and saw Rashad on the side.

But the longer I stayed with Roy, the deeper I fell for Rashad. He brought a calm to my spirit that Roy, as good a man as he was, never could. I had finally worked up the courage to end things when he popped the question, but with everyone's eyes focused on me and waiting for my answer, my nerve disappeared.

There was no way I was going to say no with a whole audience watching me. I said yes. And while everyone cheered and Roy hugged and kissed me and promised to always love me, I died.

I was in tears when I met Rashad a few days later and told him about what had happened. I figured that despite the engagement, we could continue to go on with what we had. I couldn't say no to Roy, but I wasn't willing to let Rashad go either.

Unfortunately, Rashad didn't share the same sentiment. When I told him, he went off. He said he no longer wanted to have anything to do with me.

In tears and on my knees, I begged him to give us a chance. "Please, Rashad, I need you."

"If you need me, Stacey, then go tell Roy no."

"It's not that easy, Rashad. His family . . . they were all there. I can't. Please, baby . . . we can do this."

"No, we can't, Stacey. I don't want to be the nigga on the side anymore—I'm through with that shit. Point blank, you either leave Roy so we can do this, or we're done."

"Rashad, please don't make me choose like this . . . please."

"If the choice is that hard for you, Stacey, then you're not strong enough to be the woman that I want in my life. Goodbye." Rashad left me on the floor in tears.

What he'd said was true—I wasn't strong enough. That's why I stayed with Roy, got married, had Jenea and Sheila, and pretended to be in love. All because I wasn't strong enough to admit that I wasn't.

I never thought that my marriage with Roy was going to fall apart. Although I was unhappy, I was determined to see it through until the end. I promised till death do us part, and I was sticking to that.

But when Vic left Julie, everything changed for me. Old feelings that I had locked away came back to the surface. I became bitter and angry. I was so jealous at Vic for not having children and being able to make his decision and ultimately have the type of life he wanted—that's why I didn't want him around. I couldn't bear to look at him and see the happiness emanating from him.

I invited Julie over to watch the fight because I wanted him to be as miserable as I was. I didn't want him to be there with his true love, having a good time. Yeah, it was spiteful, but for me it was necessary.

I never really thought that Roy and I would fall apart as a result of it. Though, in the back of my mind, I know I wanted that. I just didn't think I was going to get that lucky. If I could have done it a different way to avoid having Jenea and Sheila get hurt in the process, I would have.

My little angels were everything to me. They may not have been planned, but their time was due, and God had brought them to me. I just hoped that, as time went by, they would come to terms with the breakup of their home.

I sighed again as I sat down on the sofa and stared at nothing in particular. As I sat there, I realized for the first time in a long time, I was finally free.

Latrice

34

I heard the phone ringing while I was struggling to unlock the door with the bags of groceries in my hand. When I finally got it unlocked, I rushed in, grabbed the phone, and hit the talk button.

"Hello."

"Hey, LaLa."

Damn, I should have checked the caller ID. I wasted no time. "Bernard, I told you I'm seeing somebody."

Bernard huffed. "So what? Does that mean I can't call you to talk?"

I put my groceries on the counter and looked at the clock. It was seven o'clock. Vic was working late and wouldn't be home for at least another hour.

Since we were always together we'd decided that it would make more sense to pay one monthly rent. Besides, the way our relationship was progressing, we would be discussing marriage at some point, which was something we both wanted. Vic was the milk and I was the coffee; together we made one hell of a blend.

The only problem was Bernard. Since the first time he'd called me months ago, he hadn't stopped calling. He'd call me at home whenever Vic wasn't home. I don't know how, but he always knew when it was safe to call. He'd even started to call me at work, which pissed me off because I hadn't given him my number.

As hard as I tried to be a bitch, Bernard knew how to use his too-sexy voice to spit his game— game that could always make me tingle—and keep me on the phone longer than I wanted to be on. No matter how hard I tried to not let him get to me, he was doing exactly that. I found myself thinking about him when I didn't want to, hearing his voice when I was supposed to be hearing something else, seeing him when my eyes were closed. Even though I denied it, Bernard knew that he still had a hold on me.

"Look, Bernard, you know you don't just wanna talk, so don't play, okay. I told you—I am involved—"

"With Vic, the white boy. I know."

I knew Vic's color was upsetting to him and his ego, but I didn't care. "Yes, with Vic. And as you know, we live together, so I don't think he'd appreciate you calling me like this."

"LaLa, I don't care what he would or wouldn't like. I'm not concerned with him; I don't love him."

I held my breath when he said that. I didn't want to hear that word. "Bernard, you don't love me."

"You thinking for me now, LaLa?"

Exhaling frustration, I said, "I'm not thinking for you. Just telling you the truth. And don't call me LaLa anymore."

"Why? You're my LaLa. And you haven't spoken the truth yet."

Putting the groceries away, I said, "Oh really? And what truth is that?" I shook my head knowing I was falling into the web he was weaving. I tried to pull myself out of it quickly. "And I am not yours to be calling me any other names but my full name."

"The truth, LaLa," he said defiantly, "is that no matter how much you deny it and try to ignore the feeling, you and I both know that you are still feeling me. We belong together. You knew it back then, and you know it now—white boy or no white boy."

"His name is Vic, and I don't know anything right now."

"So you're not sure about him then?"

"I didn't say that."

"You just said you didn't know anything right now."

I passed my hand through my hair furiously. "Stop twisting my words around, Bernard. You know I didn't mean it like that."

"Hey, I'm only going by what I heard."

I strangled the phone. I wanted nothing more than to hang up on his ass, but for some reason I couldn't bring myself to do it. "Bernard, I got to go. My man is coming home soon, and I need to get dinner together."

"Oh, it's like that?—he's got you all domesticated and shit?"

I slammed my hand down on the counter top. Bernard was starting to irk me. "No, it's not like that! We cook for each other, just like good couples do. And I don't need to explain shit to you."

"Then why are you?" he asked matter-of-factly.

I could tell that he was smiling on the other end of the phone. "Bernard, don't call me again, okay. Just lose my number—here and at work."

"On one condition."

I broke two eggs as I was removing them from the carton to put away. "No conditions, Bernard."

"Then I can't lose your number."

Damn.

"What, Bernard . . . what the hell is your condition? What do I have to do to get you to lose my number and forget you ever knew me?" Damn, he had me worked up. I broke another egg—on purpose this time.

"Meet me for lunch tomorrow, LaLa, that's all."

"I can't do that. I've told you that before—all of the other times you asked me."

"LaLa, you've been dodging me for the past three months now. Why? I'm just asking for lunch; people do it every day."

"I'm with Vic."

"All I'm asking for is a meeting between two old friends. What's the harm in that, unless—nah, it can't be that."

"Unless what?" I asked, regretting it instantly, knowing that I'd fallen right back into the web.

"Unless you're worried that our lunch date could lead to something more. But then, you're with Vic. That wouldn't be possible."

"Damn right, it wouldn't be."

"So lunch then, say, at one?"

I sighed. "And if I have lunch with you, you'll lose my numbers, right?"

"I'll lose them as soon as you say one is on."

"Okay, Bernard, I'll entertain you. One is on."

"Cool. Meet me at Tomato Palace by the lake. Oh and, LaLa, just so you know, you entertain me every night in my thoughts."

I hung up the phone without saying a word. My heart was beating heavily and I was warm. "You should have said no, girl," I whispered to myself.

That night, as much as I didn't want to, I dreamt about Bernard.

We were making love on a bed of white roses, while the moon, in all of its splendor, glowed and illuminated our bodies. I could feel the rhythm of his body as if the music had never stopped playing. I could feel my own body sway to the groove. The dream ended in a climactic barrage of moaning and gasping so loud, I couldn't believe Vic didn't hear. But then, it was only a dream.

When the clock struck one the next day, I walked into Tomato Palace, the dream replaying in my mind. I stopped just inside the entrance and shook my head. I didn't need or want those kinds of thoughts. I walked into the main dining area and saw Bernard sitting in a booth against the wall. The Tomato Palace was one of our favorite spots to dine in when we were together. As I walked to the booth, I thought to myself, *I should have insisted on a different place.*

I sat down without saying a word.

Bernard smiled. "Mmm mmm . . . I know you said you lost all of your weight, but I didn't expect you to look the way you do now. I mean, you always looked good to me, but you definitely have worked hard. You look good, LaLa. I'm glad you finally agreed to meet me."

He tried to take my hand, but I quickly let him know I wasn't having that. "Uh uh, just remember the deal," I said seriously.

I looked at him and curled my lips. Damn, he looked good. Better than when I last saw him before our break-up. He'd put on weight—the good kind—his arms and chest were bigger, his face rounder. His weight gain looked good on his six-four frame. His hair was low and faded, and his eyes were still sleepy and sexy. And he was looking damn fine in the Hugo Boss suit he had on. I made sure not to compliment him. "I don't have long; I have a meeting to go to."

"Well, then I guess we better order."

The waiter came by a few seconds later, and we ordered our lunch. While we waited for the food, we made small talk about our jobs and our lives. Bernard told me that he'd opened up his own auto body repair shop in Laurel, and about his plans to open another in the next coming months.

I congratulated him, and told him about my growth after Danita's death. I also made sure to mention my happiness with Vic—something that, by the look on his face, he didn't want to hear.

When the food finally came, we ate in relative silence. I just wanted to eat and run and avoid his gaze, which stabbed at me like a knife. I cursed at myself silently for letting him have any type of an effect on me.

"So tell me something," he said, swallowing the last of his meal, "what does this white boy give you that you can't have with me? Because, if I recall correctly, up until you pushed me away, we had a real love thing going on."

A slow eater by nature, I was only halfway through with my spinach salad. I looked at him and shook my head. "First of all, his name is Vic—you need to start using it. Second of all, it's not about what he has; it's about the person that he is. Vic is a special man."

"He's white," Bernard cut in.

"His race doesn't mean shit to me—he makes me happy, and that's all that matters."

Taking my hand in his, Bernard said, "I used to make you happy too, or do you not remember all of that?"

I pulled my hand away. "I remember, but I'm a different person now, with different expectations, different needs, different wants."

"And you don't want me?"

"I have what I want, Bernard."

"You didn't answer my question—do you or do you not want me?" He looked at me intensely with his brown eyes. He was trying to reel me in with his gaze.

In the past, it would have worked. I would have folded and become hypnotized and powerless to his charm. And even though I still felt a little tingle for him, it was different this time. "I have the person I want, Bernard," I said resolutely.

Bernard bit on his bottom lip, leaned back in the booth and nodded slowly. "You know, I can see that you've changed. I can see that you're stronger now. Danita's death, horrible as it was, turned you into an even more beautiful person, and I don't just mean looks because, to me, you were always fine. I hear what you're saying, and I know you're for real about your feelings about your white— about Vic.

"But, I will say this—even though you are serious, and your mind is made up, I can tell that you still have feelings for me. You're not as past me as you're letting on. I can see that, even if you don't want to admit it to me, or yourself. But that's cool. I will give up on trying to take your heart back. I will respect what you have going on right now. I can be a big man and let you have your happiness, but just know, LaLa, I will always be in the shadows waiting for one more shot."

"You'll be waiting for a long time."

"We'll see."

There was a long moment of silence between us as we stared at each other. During that time, the waiter came and brought our check. Bernard paid, and then we walked out of the restaurant.

Outside, the sun was high in the sky, bringing pleasant warmth to the crisp February air.

As I slipped my hands into my gloves, Bernard looked at me. "Well, I guess this is it then."

"I guess so."

"You sure there's no chance for us to do it again?"

"Bernard," I said quietly, "I've moved on; you should too."

He took a deep breath and exhaled. "Well, do I get one last hug?"

I glared at him.

He put his hands up quickly. "All I'm asking for is a hug. One for the road, that's all."

I hesitated for a second and then nodded. "One for the road."

Bernard smiled and pulled me into him. He hugged me tightly, slowly passing his hand up and down my back.

I can't lie—it felt good to feel his arms around me. Too good. "I have to go." I pushed him away from me slowly.

To my surprise, before I could separate myself from him, he pressed his lips against mine.

At first, I tried to resist and push him away, but when he guided his tongue to my lips, my mouth instinctively opened and welcomed it inside. I met his tongue with my own and felt my body swoon. The kiss may have lasted for only a few short seconds, but it was deep, sensual, and intense.

When we finally parted, Bernard looked at me and said, "That's the answer I was looking for. I'll be in the shadows, LaLa, respectful, but waiting. Tell Vic he better not fuck it up." Without saying another word, he turned and walked away, leaving me there with hot lips and a thumping heart.

When I finally got myself calmed down, I headed to my car. Little did I know that Bernard and I weren't the only ones by the lake that day.

Julie

35

Biting down on my finger was about all I could do to keep myself from screaming when I saw Latrice kissing a man that wasn't Vic.

"That bitch!" I yelled as I drove my car down Little Patuxent Parkway. I thought back to the night she gave me her warning. "That bitch!" I yelled again, slamming my hand down on the steering wheel. *Oh, we would see whose ass gets kicked now.* "Let's see how Vic reacts to finding out about your little rendezvous."

As I waited for a red light to change, I dug my cell phone from my purse and hit speed dial one. I needed advice before I made the call. I hadn't spoken to Vic since I scratched up his car and slashed his tires, and knowing how much he loved his car, I know he had to be pissed. I was surprised he didn't call to curse me out, or worse.

I let all of my frustration out on that car. The tire slashing had been done for good measure. I wanted Vic and everyone else to know how much he hurt me and didn't regret it for a second—until now.

Latrice had just given me another chance. Somehow I had to find a way to tell Vic what I had seen. If I could find a way to make him listen to me, he'd have to realize that he was wrong about leaving me. I would make him see that we belonged together.

When Stacey answered the phone, I said, "She was kissing someone else!"

"Who?"

"That bitch that Vic is dating."

"Who? . . . Latrice?"

"Yes, La*bitch*."

"What do you mean, 'kissing someone else'? Where are you?"

"I'm on my way home right now. I took the day off today. And I mean kissing someone as in, I saw Miss Thing at the lake, giving mouth-to-mouth to some guy."

"And it wasn't Vic?"

"Unless Vic got an extremely dark tan, I'd say it wasn't him."

"Dayum, girl. You're serious? What did you do?"

Blowing the horn at an elderly driver who was doing Sunday driving on a Tuesday, I said, "Nothing. I bit down on my finger and just watched. Then I left and called you. Tell me what to do, Stacey. I can't let that bitch get away with it."

"Especially after what she said to you."

"Oh, especially after that. She thinks she got the last laugh? Not after this, she didn't. I'll be laughing all the way back into Vic's arms."

"Yeah, but what about the whole car incident? You know he's got to be pissed about that."

"I know, I know. That's why I'm calling you. Help me figure out the best way to call and tell him. Stacey, I want my man back."

"Julie—"

"Don't say it, Stacey." I pulled into my townhouse complex. "I know what you're going to say."

"Yeah, because I keep saying it—you should let Vic go. I hate to be so blunt, but he doesn't want you."

I shook my head. "He only thinks he doesn't want me, Stacey, but I know different. I can't believe that his feelings have completely gone away like that. No matter how hard he tries to act like they have, I can't believe it. He was confused, that's all. And you can be sure Latrice did whatever she could to keep him confused. Think about it—they met at work—do you honestly think she wasn't trying to put the moves on him when she first met him? She was probably screwing with his head from day one. That's why Vic changed his mind about us, not because he fell out of love with me; she just got to him."

"Julie, I hear what you're saying, but—"

"Stacey, I love you, and I appreciate your friendship, but I don't want to hear any buts. I just know Vic isn't over me, that's all that matters. I'll show you, him, and everyone else. Now, I called you to ask for advice on how to tell him. Are you going to give me that advice or not?"

Stacey didn't say anything for a few seconds.

I started to worry that maybe I had been too crude, but I couldn't help it. The last thing I wanted to hear was that Vic was not in love with me anymore. I'd been hearing that for too long, and at one point I almost believed it myself. But that night at Roy and Stacey's, I overheard him and Colin in the kitchen. He was worried about who Derrick was. If he were over me, he would never have cared about who I was with.

I shut off my engine and sat still for a few seconds. I pictured Latrice kissing her mystery man. I wanted to paint that very picture for Vic.

"So are you going to help me, Stacey?"

Stacey started to say something, but then she sighed. "Okay, girl, if you really want to do this . . ."

Before leaving my car, Stacey and I figured out a way to break the news to Vic. I smiled the biggest smile I had in a long time, and I had no one but Latrice to thank for it.

Vic

36

I sat across from Julie at the Macaroni Grill restaurant and stared at her. It was packed with diners, and endless conversation filtered through the air. No one seemed to notice or care that we weren't speaking.

Not really wanting to be there, I'd arrived twenty minutes late. After all the bullshit she'd pulled lately, she was lucky I didn't go off on her when she called me at work and asked to meet for lunch. After her performance with my car, I'd already had enough people at work in my business, and the last thing I needed was for anyone to hear me losing my cool on the phone with her. That's why I agreed to meet her.

While we were on the phone, she'd tried to apologize, saying she had a lot of explaining to do, but I couldn't have cared less about her apology. I only agreed to the lunch meeting because I had something to make clear once and for all. So there I sat, while the ice melted in my glass, everyone around us having a good time. I watched Julie with cold eyes. I wanted her to see how angry I was. From the way she played with her napkin and kept her eyes focused everywhere else but on me, I could tell that she knew.

After the waiter came around and took my to-go order, I took a sip of water and cleared my throat. "Julie, I really don't care about what you have to say to me, okay. I only agreed to meet you because I want to make one thing clear to you."

Before I could say anything else, Julie put up her hand. "Vic, before you go on, let me apologize again for the scene I caused at your job, and what I did to your car—it was wrong of me to do that."

I clenched my jaws. I was trying to avoid talking about that, because just the thought of that day made my blood boil.

Julie stared at me, waiting for me to respond.

I took a deep breath and tried to calm down.

"Julie, that shit you did cost me close to two thousand dollars to fix. Add that to the embarrassment I felt at work, and you'll understand when I say I don't want to hear any of your damn apologies." I shivered from the chill in my own voice.

She looked at me and exhaled. "Why did you agree to come then, Vic?" she asked, tightening her lips.

"Look, I just want to make one thing clear to you, Julie—I'm not in love with you."

"Vic—"

"I've told you already, Julie, I'm sorry you're hurting. Like I've said, I don't take pleasure in it, but we both deserve to be happy. And that wouldn't have happened if I had stayed with you. Now, please, don't call me anymore. Just stay the hell away from me and my car." I stood up to leave. I wanted to go before I lost my cool.

"Are you in love with her, Vic?" Julie asked, before I could step away.

I looked at her. "Yes."

"And do you think she's in love with you?"

"What?"

"Do you think she's in love with you?" Julie asked again, this time with a smirk.

I could feel the eyes of some of the diners focused on us. I gave one gentleman a look that let him know what business he should have been minding. I looked down at Julie. "Yes." I turned my back to leave.

Then Julie said loud enough for me and everyone else to hear. "If she's in love with you, why was she kissing another man?"

I turned around and asked in a heated whisper, "What did you say?"

"Ask your bitch who the black man was that she was kissing yesterday afternoon by the lake."

I stared at her. "What the fuck did you say?"

She returned my glare with her own. "That bitch who you say you are in love with, the one who you say is in love with you, was busy taking in another man's saliva yesterday in front of Tomato Palace—I saw it with my own eyes, Vic; make sure she knows that."

Unable to keep my voice down, and not really caring, I sat down. "Aren't you tired of the fucking games, Julie? Haven't you done enough shit already? Haven't you caused enough damage? Do you take pleasure in being a bitch?"

"Just ask her, Vic," Julie said with cool confidence. "And when you find out, let me know. Maybe then we can work on us."

Without another word, she stood up from the table and walked past me out of the restaurant.

I sat silent while everyone's eyes were focused solely on me. I felt like I was E.F. Hutton and everyone was ready to listen to what I had to say. I didn't say a word. I just sat unmoving, digesting what Julie told me. *Was she playing another one of her games? Could Latrice really have done what Julie said she did?* There was only one way to find out.

Leaving my food on the table, I walked out of the restaurant and hit speed dial two on my cell phone. When Latrice's voice mail clicked on, I left a simple message. "I'm not coming back to work. We'll talk when I see you tonight."

Latrice

37

From the moment I listened to the message Vic left for me, I knew something was wrong. I tried to call him, to find out what he wanted to talk about, or at least to get some type of heads-up, but he never answered his cell. When I tried the house, I got the same results. I didn't even bother to go to the gym, because I couldn't focus.

The tone in his voice was so cold. *What could've been on his mind?* Our relationship was as strong as ever and was getting stronger with each passing day, so it couldn't have anything to do with us. Something must have happened. Well, if that was the case, I would make sure to cheer him up the best way I could. That's why I stopped at Victoria's Secret on the way home—Vic was my man, and my man sounded like he needed to be cheered up. I figured a sexy, new outfit would be just the thing to lift his spirits.

I stepped through the front door, ready and willing to do all of the cheering he could take. I had the fire-red, crotchless panties, garter, and open-nipple bra set on underneath my business suit. As horny as I was, and as turned on as I planned to make him, I figured our talk would last all of five minutes.

"Hey, baby," I said, putting down my laptop case and walking into the living room.

Vic sat stone-still in his favorite chair with a beer bottle in his hand and didn't say a word to me. He stared past me in the dead silence of the living room.

I walked over to him and gave him a kiss on the lips, but he never moved his mouth. He continued to stare at nothing in particular.

"So what's up, baby? I got your message about not going back to work. You said you wanted to talk. Did something happen at work today? . . . because if that's the case, I have just the thing to replace that sour look with a big smile." I straddled his legs and kissed him on the forehead.

To my surprise, Vic never moved nor got aroused.

"Vic, what's wrong?"

Finally waking from his trance, he took a swallow of his beer and, without warning, stood, causing me to almost fall.

"What the hell! What is your problem?"

He put down the bottle on a side table and turned toward me. His blue eyes were the blackest I'd ever seen. "Where did you go for lunch yesterday?" he asked quietly. He focused on me and waited for an answer.

My heart started beating heavily as I studied his eyes and tried to buy some time. *Does he know about*

Bernard? How? "Lunch. I went out with a couple of girlfriends."

"A couple of girlfriends, huh? Who?"

"Just a couple of girls from the office. They work in one of the other buildings, so you wouldn't know them."

"Where did you guys go?" he asked, his eyes never blinking.

"We just went out for a quick bite to eat. What's with all of these questions?"

"So, you didn't go to Tomato Palace for lunch then?"

Shit! "What's up with these questions?"

"Just answer my question!" he yelled, his voice rising in a way I'd never heard.

I tried to keep my composure, although I was worried. "No, you didn't just yell at me like that. You know better than to talk to me that way, Vic— you know I don't play."

"Then tell me the fuckin' truth, Latrice!" He turned and grabbed his beer bottle and finished it off. "You know what—don't say anything, because I already know."

"What are you talking about?" I asked in a whisper of a voice.

"I have a friend who works at Tomato Palace. Remember Shantal, one of the waitresses there? She saw you. She was just walking in from the back and saw you leaving with some guy. A guy who wasn't me."

I exhaled. *Damn.* "So what . . . she decided to call you up and tell you? Yes, I was there, okay—is that what you want to hear?"

"I want the truth, Latrice, that's all, the god-damned truth."

"Vic, I don't know what she told you, but it's not even close to being as bad as you think it is."

Vic gave a half-smile, sat down in the chair, rested his elbows on his knees, and intertwined his fingers. "Actually, Latrice, Shantal didn't tell me much at all. She just said that you were there. She's not the one who saw you lip-locked with whoever the fuck you were with. The sad and embarrassing truth is that Julie was the one who saw that shit. And believe me, she didn't hesitate to give me the details."

I bit down on my lip and shook my head. "Vic, believe me, whatever that bitch said, it wasn't true; you know how she feels about me."

"Oh, so you weren't kissing anybody?"

Damn. I sat down and passed my hands through my hair. I could feel my skin tingling and my hands shaking. *Julie . . . that bitch was going to get it.* I took a deep breath and tried to hold myself together. *Damn, Julie. Damn, Bernard.*

"So which is it, Latrice—were you, or were you not kissing somebody? And who the fuck was he anyway?"

I sighed. I knew that I had to tell the truth. I just hoped he would believe me. "Yes," I started in a weak voice, "I kissed him, but it's not what you think."

"Who was he?"

Shit. I knew the minute I mentioned Bernard's name, Vic was going to fly off the handle. "It was Bernard."

Within seconds, Vic was standing erect, and his voice boomed. "Bernard . . . your ex? What the fuck! Latrice, tell me this is some kind of fuckin' joke."

I stood up and approached him, but he backed away from me. "Vic, it's not what you think, for real. Let me explain."

"'Explain'? What the fuck could you possibly explain to me? You met your ex for lunch, and then you had your tongue down his throat—what more is there to say?"

"Vic, *he* kissed *me*! It's not what you think."

"So what . . . you felt you had to kiss him back? I don't believe this shit! And you even had the nerve to try and lie to me about this shit! Just tell me one thing, Latrice—how long has this been going on? Damn!" Vic turned around and swatted the empty beer bottle off the table, causing it to fly against the wall and shatter into pieces. Not since the night at Roy's had I seen him so angry.

I took a cautious step backwards. "Vic, I'm sorry about lying to you, okay, but please . . . believe me when I say it wasn't as bad as Julie may have made it seem."

Turning to face me, he said, "Latrice, you kissed him—isn't that bad enough?"

"Please, baby . . . I told you, *he* kissed *me*, and it didn't last. I pushed him away; he knows where I stand."

"He obviously didn't care about where you stood when his lips were locked on yours. How the hell did you hook up with him anyway? And you never answered—how long has this been going on?"

"Vic, first of all, nothing is going on. He's been calling me for the past couple of months, trying to hook up with me. I kept turning him down."

"And what happened this time?"

"This time I agreed to meet him for lunch, only if he agreed to leave me alone. Vic, I love you and he knows that—that is the truth. The kiss meant nothing. I promise you that."

Vic stared at me and breathed heavily.

I pleaded with him with my eyes. "Nothing is going on with me and Bernard; I just wanted him to leave me alone."

"So what . . . you couldn't tell me about it?"

"I handled it the best way I could."

"'The best way,' huh? What a way—you meet him for lunch, chitchat for a few, and then exchange a goodbye kiss. To make matters worse, of all people, Julie had to see that shit. Goddamn!" He turned away from me and placed his hands on top of his head. His back to me, he said, "I got to get the fuck out of here."

Before I could respond, he turned, stormed past me and left, leaving me there, pissed and scared.

Julie was going to get hers—that was for sure. But had I lost Vic?

Colin

38

For the first time in my life, I was really in love. I don't know how it happened, and I sure as hell didn't plan on it happening. But it did. I was in love with Emily. Somehow, she'd managed to get a hold of my heart and claim it as hers, and I had absolutely no problem with that. My player's card had been thrown away, and I was cool with that. I didn't want to be in the game any longer.

Emily was my better half. Better still, she was my friend. I had never had a friend like her before. I could talk to her about anything, and that's what I loved about her. Add to that the fact that she was fine and could work enough magic in the bedroom to keep me under her spell, and her race became a non-existent factor.

That's why I bought the engagement ring. I had found my ONE. I knew that, with her, we could work through any and all problems. The nice thing was I didn't foresee too many problems ahead in our future together. We'd have our arguments, of course, but I knew we would never have issues like Roy and Stacey, or Latrice and Vic.

Speaking of which, I couldn't believe what had happened between Vic and Latrice. When Vic came by the other night and told me about Latrice and her ex and that Julie had seen the whole thing, I wasn't entirely surprised. After everything Stacey and Julie had done, it wasn't hard to believe that Latrice could do some shit too. *Women.*

Once again, Vic was camping out at my spot. *Damn, who said that my place was going to be a boarding house for fools in love?* But I didn't really mind. I was there for my boys whenever they needed me. Besides, I was always with Emily.

We'd started talking about getting a place together; we both wanted a house. We'd dabbled with the subject of marriage, but I always acted like I wasn't ready for it. Emily was cool with that. She was willing to be patient and not put the pressure on me—that's why I knew she'd be blown away when I popped the question.

I had it all planned out. I was going to take her back to where we first met, Angelo and Maxie's Steakhouse, treat her to anything she wanted on the menu, and then take her to Zanzibar, where I didn't dance with her that first time. This time I would make sure we got our groove on. Then, when the DJ switched up the music and threw on "Ribbon in the Sky," by Stevie Wonder, I would get down on one knee and propose to her. I had it all hooked up—my boy was the DJ there, and I'd already gone over the plan with him.

I wanted to propose at Zanzibar because I wanted Emily to see how serious I was about her.

She always knew about my apprehensions because of her color, so I figured if I did it like that, then she would understand that I didn't give two shits about anyone's feelings but hers. Yeah, I was ready.

I just hoped Latrice and Vic could get their shit settled. Vic told me everything that Latrice had told him, and although it was a messed up thing to do, I knew from experience how it could have happened. I knew Latrice really loved Vic, and so did Emily. She spoke to Latrice and got the low-down from her; Latrice wouldn't lie to her girl. We told Vic about how meaningless the kiss actually was, but as a man, knowing that your woman was kissing another man can be a bitter pill to swallow.

I can't front, though—Latrice definitely should have told him about the phone calls so that Vic could have put to rest anything Bernard was trying to do. But she didn't, and now Vic was upset, and Latrice was sad.

I knew they would get past it. Those two loved each other, and it was going to take something more serious than a moment of weakness to break them apart, just like with Emily and me. That's why I was humming to myself as I drove home. I was happy. The feeling I had inside made me realize how much of a fool my father was, and how much of a fool I was for following in his footsteps. I wouldn't do to Emily what my father did to my mother—I was going to walk down that aisle.

Latrice

39

I was so hurt when Vic walked out and didn't come home for a few days. I couldn't even go to work—I was that depressed. I actually thought I was going to lose him. My fear only lessened a little when he finally came home. Even then, things were still shaky, because he didn't speak to me much.

Eventually though, we did speak and found a way to work out our problems over my mistake with Bernard. Thankfully, Emily and Colin both helped him to understand that my mistake was just that and nothing more.

Our issue may have been resolved, but there was still something I needed to take care of. I knew what Julie's game was the minute Vic told me she was the one who gave him the information—she wanted him back, and I wasn't having that.

I wasn't about to let her get away with what she tried to do. She had crossed the line. That's why I found out where she lived, and now I was ringing on her doorbell. *She is going to get hers.* I felt like Jill Scott in her video, "Gettin' in the Way." I had my earrings off and my hands ready. When she opened the door, the first and only thing I could say was, "Bitch, I warned you that night!"

Julie screamed out and tried to shut the door, but I wasn't having it. I wasn't leaving until she knew that I never made empty threats. She'd brought the ugly out in me, and it wasn't going back in until my flesh touched hers.

I put my foot in-between the doorway to keep the door from closing, and then pushed my way inside.

Julie screamed again and backed into her living room. "Get out of my house, you bitch!"

I laughed. "No, *you* didn't just call *me* a bitch. Did you really think your plan was going to work? Did you really think that you were going to get Vic back?" I rushed at her, but had to stop to avoid a lamp she threw at me.

"You don't love Vic!"

"How are you gonna tell me who I love?" I asked as I watched her pick up another lamp. "You're the one who doesn't love him. If you did, you would never have tried that shit at Roy's house, and you certainly wouldn't have scratched up his car."

"He deserves better than you!"

"And what . . . you think you're better? Bitch, please . . . the only thing you proved by running to Vic with what you saw and didn't understand was that you are a vindictive, jealous bitch."

"Vic does love me. You just brainwashed him and made him think he loves you."

"So I'm a hypnotist now."

Julie threw another lamp at me, missing me by a mile.

I could only laugh. "That's real smart, Julie—break your shit up."

"Get out of my house, or I'll call the police."

I watched her and huffed. "Oh, you would do that. So you can dish out your shit, but you can't take it, huh?"

As Julie scrambled around her couch to reach for something else to throw, I charged at her, grabbed her by her arm, and spun her around. Without hesitating, I gave her one hell of a smack. It stung my palm.

Julie cried out but, to my surprise, retaliated with a smack of her own, and it actually hurt.

"Oh no, you didn't." I grabbed her hair and dragged her to the ground while she swiped at me.

We wrestled there, exchanging slaps and scratches. It had been a while since I'd been in a catfight, but I hadn't forgotten how to kick a bitch's ass. I savored every smack I gave her. Finally, after a couple more hits, I got up and stood over her.

As she cried quietly, I touched my cheek, which she'd scratched. I sucked on the blood coming from my split lip. Even though I'd gotten the best of her, she'd surprised me with her toughness.

"Hear me good, Julie—you had your chance with Vic, and you lost out. Stay the hell away from my man. Oh, and before you get any ideas about running to him about what just happened, let me just tell you—he knew I was coming over here, and he also knew better than to try and stop me—that's how much he loves you, Julie."

I turned around and walked away and went back home to my man. Julie never bothered us again after that.

Colin

40

It was my wedding day, and I couldn't have been any happier.

The night I proposed to Emily went exactly the way I'd planned it, with a little extra surprise thrown in. We went to the restaurant and ate up a storm. Actually, Emily ate up a storm, while I just picked at my food. I was nervous—that was the last thing I thought I was going to be. We ate and talked for a while, and after Emily got another order of chicken strips to go, we went to Zanzibar.

We danced like we'd never danced. It wasn't our first time dancing together, but it felt different for me. I was dancing with my lady and didn't care about the nasty glares the sisters were giving me. I know Emily didn't care, because she was too busy shaking that ass.

After I gave my cue to the DJ, he slowed things down. I held Emily close as the slow jams played.

Then, when my song came on, I dropped down to one knee. A spotlight was placed on us, and everybody in the club got quiet. I looked up at Emily, tears snaking from her eyes. While Stevie sang, I said, "Emily, you know what kind of man I am, and you know it takes a special woman for me to do something like this. Well, you are that special woman, and I want everyone here and everywhere else to know that." I removed the ring box from my pocket and opened it. Everyone, including the sisters, gasped at the two-carat ring I offered.

Emily's bottom lip quivered as I held her hand. "Em, it was here when you first called me out and kept it real. I want to do the same now; I want to keep it real with you. Will you marry me?"

She screamed out and pulled me up to her with strength I didn't know she had. She kissed me furiously. "Yes! Yes! Yes!"

Applause erupted around the club. Even the sisters were clapping. When the spotlight went off, the DJ replayed the song for us. We danced and held each other tightly, while the floor slowly filled with other couples.

Like I said, the night went exactly as I had planned, but as Emily and I danced, I got a surprise I hadn't been expecting. "I'm pregnant," she whispered in my ear.

I looked at her. "As in a baby?"

She smiled. "As in Mommy and Daddy."

"As in a family," I whispered, kissing her deeply. I was happy and content.

*   *   *

My wife rested her head on my shoulder, and I looked over at my best men, who were sitting by the wedding party's table, smiling at me and shaking their heads.

I'd waited a couple of days before telling them about my proposal. It was our weekly pool night at the Havana Club. "Dogs, I have somethin' to tell y'all. You guys may want to sit down."

They both looked at me with worry in their eyes.

I laughed and said, "It's not that serious."

Racking up the balls for the next game, Roy said, "What's up, man?"

"Yeah, what's with wanting us to sit down?" Vic added.

I looked at my boys and smiled. "I proposed to Emily last weekend."

They looked at me with open-mouthed stares.

I shrugged my shoulders. "We didn't say anything yet because I wanted to tell you guys this way. She's tellin' Latrice tonight."

Neither Roy nor Vic said anything for a couple seconds; in fact, neither one of them moved.

Finally, I said, "So . . . y'all gonna congratulate a brother or what?"

They both moved at last, and then Roy spoke. "You for real?"

I nodded my head and smiled. "As real as Halle is fine."

Vic stepped toward me. "You mean, you *proposed*, as in no more playa-playa?"

"Oh, I'll always be a playa, but just with one woman now. Fellas, I'm ready to settle down. Emily is the one for me."

In unison, they both said, "Dayum!"

Then I hit them again. "One more thing—I'm going to be a father; Em told me after I proposed."

Again in unison, "Dayum!"

Vic gave me a pound. "Congratulations, man. You sure you're ready for this?"

"Yeah," Roy added, giving me a pound of his own, "marriage and kids are a big deal, man."

"Dogs, I am ready and excited."

"I can't believe the playa of the year is heading to the altar," Vic said.

"Believe it," I beamed.

When the waitress came around, we ordered three glasses of champagne and toasted to my happiness.

We toasted to that again as they made their speeches during the beginning of the reception.

I had to have both of them as best men; they were my brothers for life. I gave a subtle nod to both of them and then put all of my attention back on my wife.

Roy

41

When the judge brought the gavel down to pass sentence, I forced myself to remain composed. Despite Stacey's attempts to get full custody, the judge, a disgruntled-looking white woman with iron-gray hair, awarded me partial custody of Jenea and Sheila. Stacey, who had moved back home to Tennessee, would have the girls during the school year, while I had them all to myself for the summer months.

I wanted to walk up to the judge, kiss her wrinkled cheeks, and give her petite frame a tight squeeze, but I knew better. Instead, I sat quiet until she exited the chambers. Then I thanked my attorney, a short black man, whose name ironically enough, was Johnni Cockran, and then gathered my jacket to leave.

Before I did, I walked over to where Stacey was still sitting, speechless and unmoved, even after her attorney had already left. I tried to keep back my smile, but it was damn hard to do. Stacey had done so much wrong that I felt the judge's decision was more than fair. If it had been up to me, Stacey wouldn't be seeing my little girls at all; I still harbored ill feelings for the things she'd done.

It didn't make matters any better when I found out she had been cheating on me prior to us even getting married. Her mother revealed that secret. She told me all about how she saw Stacey sneaking off with him after I had dropped her off one day.

When I asked her how come she never told me, she said, "Because she's my daughter."

"And why are you telling me this now?"

"Because you are my son-in-law. Always will be."

I didn't say anything else, and neither did Mrs. Bolton. She loved her daughter, but she was disappointed in her. I was glad that I would still be able to call her family.

I looked at Stacey. She kept her eyes focused on the judge's empty chair. I know she didn't expect the verdict to have gone that way, especially after trying to paint an ugly picture of me in court. She and her lawyer tried to make it seem as though I were a bad father with wild ways and unscrupulous friends. The judge obviously saw through their BS.

"Stacey," I said quietly, "I hope we'll be able to raise our girls with as little conflict as possible. The judge made her decision; I hope you plan on respecting that."

Stacey said nothing, but she did turn her gaze up at me.

I added, "I only want what's best for the girls."

Stacey stood up and continued to stare at me as though I were the devil incarnate. Finally, she gathered her purse and jacket and said, "I'll be by to pick the girls up in a couple of months." Then she walked past me and out of the courtroom without another word.

I let my smile bloom when the doors closed behind her. Then I turned and faced Keisha Wilkins. She and I had been seeing each other for the past six months. She had strong feelings for me, and I knew they were genuine.

She smiled and approached me. "Congratulations," she whispered as she kissed me softly.

I kissed her back and held her close.

Keisha and I met when she had come to purchase a car. The attraction was immediate for both of us. By the end of her shopping excursion, she drove off in a brand-new Toyota Camry and left her phone number.

We started dating soon after that, and when my little girls finally met her and gave her a thumbs-up, I felt like God had answered my prayers. Keisha would never replace Stacey, something I wouldn't have allowed to happen anyway, but Jenea and Sheila respected her and loved her a great deal.

I was proud of the way my girls handled the turmoil and stress, and adapted to the new situation. Throughout the entire ordeal, my girls showed me how mature they were. They knew and understood that their Mommy and Daddy weren't happy together, and our happiness was all they wanted. Unselfishly, they pushed for me to be with Keisha.

I took Keisha's hand and squeezed it gently. "Let's go pick up the girls."

Vic

42

Roy had his new love, Keisha, and had won partial custody of his daughters; Colin had Emily and a baby on the way; and I had Latrice, who I would be proposing to as soon as I found the perfect ring. Life, however, as ugly as it seemed sometimes, had turned out to be damn good. Latrice and I were stuck with each other, and neither one of us had a problem with that. We were both happy.

Latrice's announcement to me one night over dinner only made things better. "Vic, I'm pregnant."

I stared at her for a long, quiet minute after she said that. The news was just what I wanted to hear. "We having a boy or a girl?" I replied.

"We won't be able to find out for a couple more months, but I don't want to know; I want to be surprised. Are you okay with the news?" She looked at me through semi-worried eyes; she knew all about Julie and the miscarriage.

I smiled, stood up, and approached her. I took

her hands in my own. As she stood tall, I placed my hand on her flat belly and imagined feeling the first kick in a couple of months. "We need to hurry and get this one out of there."

"Why is that?"

I smiled and kissed her nose. "Because then we can get started on the next one."

"Oh, is that right?" she asked, slitting her eyes playfully.

I smiled. "You know it."

We both laughed and held each other in a tight embrace. I held her and could never imagine letting her go.

Colin and Roy were my best men for the second and final time, when Latrice and I said our "I do's" before our first son was born.

We had two more boys after that. This time, I had no doubts.